PARANORMAL CLUB

A NOVEL BY
SIR PATRICK BIJOU

DESCRIPTION

Do You Want to Spice up Your Night with a Racy and Arousing Story That Will Thrill You at the Same Time? Paranormal Club is a thrilling erotic horror story that will offer you that and much more!

A private college in American Midwest... Supernatural experience that first manifested as a vivid dream...
John is a member of a Paranormal Club, an unofficial ghost-hunting club, because the college he attended wouldn't let some outlandish claims of supernatural tarnish their reputation.

Unlike other students that spend their Friday nights binge drinking, the members of PC spent those nights exploring decrepit old buildings with a variety of recording equipment, trying to catch evidence of supernatural activity on tape.

Even though they had fun, they have never gotten any sort of evidence that couldn't have been faked by an unscrupulous attention-seeker, until John started to have these incredibly vivid and erotic dreams.

Enchanted by the vivid dreams, John gets drawn into a thrilling nightmarish game where the stakes get higher and higher each time…What will be the cost of John's curiosity?

Thrilling and thought-provoking, Paranormal Club is a naughty and saucy, erotic horror story that will take you on a captivating journey that will always keep you on your toes. With every turn of the page, your mind and heart will yearn for more… So what are you waiting for?

ABOUT THE AUTHOR

Sir Patrick's journey into content writing has allowed him to become an exceptionally motivated and enthusiastic author and professional communicator. Experienced in both proactive campaign-driven and responsive communications.

He is an eclectic writer, lives in the United Kingdom and was born in Georgetown and raised in London, England. His diverse writing prowess has been influenced by many experiences. He pursued several courses of study at several universities and declared two majors during his schooling which included the areas of Business and Economics and finally obtained his doctorate in Economics and International banking.
In all these scholastic studies though, the true treasures he took away are not the certificates (though those are very important), but instead, the experiences he had, the people he met, the foods he ate and even the places he stayed.

"In truth, he is a citizen of the world and this has greatly influenced his writing.

So, if you are already a fan, I appreciate you. If you are not yet one, then what are you waiting for? Read a book and then read some more. I create characters that resonate with you and infuse life into all I write".

Sir Patrick has written over 20 published fictional and non-fictional books across several genres. He writes for the liberation of all people, focusing on those who are often left out the literary world of creative writing.

Thank you again for purchasing this book, I hope you have enjoyed it!

My name is John, and I attend a small, respectable private college in the American Midwest. Most people have no clue that our college has a ghost-hunting club, and the powers-that-be in our obscure little slice of American academia wish to keep it that way. For the sake of maintaining the respectability of our Alma Mater, the "paranormal research club" (as we describe ourselves) isn't listed as an official on-campus organization. Our unofficial faculty adviser, Professor Morrison, is a well-respected authority on 18th century English Romantic poetry, and the author of several widely circulated books on the subject. She possesses enough tenure and seniority at the university that her famous idiosyncrasies and peccadilloes are largely ignored or tolerated by the other faculty members, and she also just happens to be the niece of a former dean as well as the daughter of one of the school's biggest financial contributors. It was unequivocally understood that her eventual retirement would mark the end of any association, official or otherwise, between our university and anything as potentially embarrassing to the academic community as paranormal research. In the meanwhile, however, while other students spend their Friday nights out binge drinking or buried beneath research projects, the seven to ten of us that routinely attend the paranormal club meetings would spend our nights exploring decrepit old buildings with a variety of recording equipment, trying to catch evidence of supernatural activity on tape. We usually have a bunch of fun doing it, and it's really a neat feeling when you catch a recording of something that you can't rationally explain and you get to share it triumphantly with your friends over beer and pizza.

We've never gotten any sort of evidence that couldn't have been faked by an unscrupulous attention-seeker, but most of the people in our club aren't out to convince the rest of the world that ghosts, hauntings, or anything else supernatural really exists. Ghost hunting can be an expensive hobby, even when you make do with relatively inexpensive equipment, but it's a hobby that we enjoy for its own sake. People are pretty much just going to believe what they choose to believe regarding the paranormal, and that's fine with us. We're all pretty good friends, and in reality, our paranormal researchgives us an excuse to go around playing in creepy old abandoned buildings and hang out together.

It was Spring Break of last year, and one of the members of the club had spent most of the previous three years trying to persuade us to make the 13 hour trip to do an investigation at the church in southern Vermont where her father had been the pastor for the past 19 years. Erin was a petite, willowy young woman with sparkling green eyes, adorable freckles, and long brown hair. She was a senior this year majoring in Speech Pathology. As a senior, she viewed this year as her last chance to make an investigation of her father's church happen. She told us that her interest in joining our paranormal club had been sparked by an entire childhood surrounded by the mysterious goings-on at that ancient house of prayer.

Erin was a bit of an anomaly in our club. She was deeply religious, and she seldom failed to be at the local church she attended multiple times a week unless she was deathly ill. She wasn't pushy with her religion, but she was a virgin and planned to stay that way until she was married. It was hard to imagine her staying single for long. She was physically attractive, easy going, and she had a cheerful and good-natured personality that frequently lit her face up with a brilliant smile. She was just the sort of woman that any young man that was considering marriage might do well to pursue if the idea of having a large family didn't scare him off. Erin's family didn't appear to be rich, but I often suspected that she was descended from old money based on stray bits of conversation that I gathered over the years. Both my sister and I liked Erin a great deal as a friend.

While organized religion generally tends to be skeptical at best when it comes to paranormal investigators such as ourselves, Erin's father had enthusiastically welcomed the idea of us doing an investigation at his church. Over the phone, he and his wife had told stories of ghostly sounds, smells, objects moving on their own, and sights including full-body apparitions that rivaled the activity reported to occur in some of the most haunted castles in Europe. Lots of people exaggerate what goes on in a haunted house, sometimes because they're frightened and other times because they want attention. Erin assured us that, if anything, her father was downplaying what went on in the old church in an effort to keep his stories from sounding too outrageous and difficult to believe. We had known her long enough and had been on enough investigations with her that none of us doubted her truthfulness. Perhaps, out of the entire club, the biggest supporter of Erin's idea of investigating the old church was Dr. Morrison herself, which was unusual. Dr. Morrison was always supportive of our efforts, but she seldom did anything to push us one way or another on a project.

The fact that Erin could vouch for everyone in our club's character had encouraged her father in his decision to enlist our aid, just as our faith in Erin's word had made us willing to make such a long trip. Her father, David, wished to avoid local notoriety and not earn his church any more of a supernatural reputation than it already had. The fact that we were all from out- of-state and might be able to verify what he and his family routinely saw, without compromising the local reputation of his venerable house of worship, was an absolute godsend from his perspective. He offered to pay for the fuel that our large gas-guzzling van full of people and equipment would need to get there and back, which was no small gesture. In addition, he and his wife were willing to put us up in his home and feed us home-cooked meals while we were there, so there would be no need to pay for hotel rooms or meals. If Erin's mother, Naomi, was even half the cook that Erin described her as being then it was worth the trip for the food alone. David had generously offered to pay us each for our time, but through Erin we politely declined payment because we never take money from any interested party when we are researching a site. For a bunch of broke college kids with an interest in the paranormal, the whole trip appeared to be a remarkably good deal, and Dr. Morrison seemed almost as happy as Erin that we would be able to go. It sounded like fun, and everyone liked Erin enough that it was no problem getting the club to commit to the investigation, much to her and her parents' joy.

It was the night before we were scheduled to leave for our adventure in Vermont. Steve and Frank, two Industrial Design majors that you could just about always count on being a part of any adventure that the club participated in, were renting an old farmhouse about thirty minutes away from campus. On our investigations, we usually all drove to their house, loaded the equipment that we kept in their garage into a battered old van that we kept parked there, and then everyone rode in the van to wherever we were going to investigate. Their house provided us with a natural staging area, and everyone had agreed to meet at Steve and Frank's abode at 6:30 the next morning, load the van just like we always did, and hit the road at 7:00 sharp. We would drive in shifts, and hopefully we would reach Erin's parents' house between eleven o' clock at night and midnight. All six of our most experienced members had volunteered to go, which would be just enough people to effectively pull off a good investigation of the scope that the old church deserved.

Before going to sleep on the night before we were to leave, I carefully ensured that I had set my alarm clock for 5:30, and as always, I set my cell phone's built in alarm to go off ten minutes later should the primary alarm clock fail. Back when I was enlisted in the Army, I had gotten into the habit of always setting a backup alarm in case my primary alarm stopped working for any reason, and the system had never failed me. I had the large internal-frame hiking rucksack that I used for my personal luggage at the foot of my bed, already packed and ready to go. I had my cargo pants laid out for the next day on my nightstand, the pockets already loaded so that all I had to do was pull the clothing on the next morning. Again, that was a habit I picked up when I was in the Army during those times when I had the luxury of sleeping undressed. I laid out a comfortable t-shirt, a pair of socks, and my favorite insulated vest to make sure I didn't forget it. Even when it's warm outside, it can get chilly when you're ghost hunting at night, and vests are also great for the extra pockets they provide. I've always been a firm believer that you can never have too many pockets. Pulling my soft flannel sheets over myself, I quickly drifted off to sleep.

My dreams that night were both deeply disturbing and extremely erotic at once. In my dream, I was lying naked in the center of a large, circular clearing in a forest of immense and ancient trees. High above me, the stars twinkled and the full moon shone down brightly. The grassy clearing was brightly lit by moonlight and blazing torches, but the light seemed to end abruptly at the tree line, as though it could no longer sustain itself among the twisted and moss- covered branches of the dense, fog-shrouded woods. I had the distinct feeling that I was here as some sort of sacrificial offering. Strangely, the thought didn't bother me. I didn't think that I was bound, but my arms and legs hardly responded at all to any efforts I made to move them. I couldn't turn my head at all. It was a rather helpless feeling, but it was more annoying than frightening. Lying beneath me, I could feel a naked woman cradling me comfortably against her abdomen and chest, her warm skin comfortable against my back and her soft breasts nestled against my shoulders. Even though I had no clue who she was, it was still a comforting feeling to have her against me.

I was surrounded on all sides by a large ring of women that were dancing naked and barefoot on the soft green grass to the sound of discordant pipe music and sensually rhythmic drumbeats. Some of the women I recognized: friends, family members, even professors and classmates from college were among those present. Many other women looked entirely unfamiliar, but most of them looked like ordinary, everyday women that I would not expect to be taking part in the pagan dance that I saw occurring around me. Women of all ages, descriptions, and body types, and all of them completely nude and covered in sweat that glistened and reflected the flickering torchlight were pressing towards me in a tightening ring of dancing flesh, their bodies moving in a manner that seemed to mimic the flickering flames of the burning torches. Something seemed to be driving them and energizing them in a manner that imbued even the least athletic-looking among them with sufficient stamina for them to effortlessly exert themselves with tremendous vigor. Slowly, the ring of women began to tighten around me as they danced. Around and around they whirled and cavorted, closer and closer they came until I could hear their breathing and see every detail, every soft body hair, and every drop of sultry sweat on the glistening female bodies. My painfully erect penis strained upward like a stone obelisk, and my heart pounded within my chest as adrenaline and testosterone coursed through my veins.

Lying immobile on the ground, I soon felt hot, sweaty female flesh pressing and writhing against me from all directions, rubbing softly along every part of my body. The woman beneath me was now feverishly grinding her sopping wet vulva against the small of my back, her small, firm breasts rubbing against my shoulder blades from behind. I felt her chest rise and fall as her hot breath became heavier against the back of my neck, and I could even feel her heartbeat pounding against my back. I wanted to turn to see who she was, but my body refused to obey me. Everywhere I was surrounded by a seething mass of anonymous female flesh, warm, soft, moist, enticing, and writhing against me. The air was thick with the smell of incense, clean sweat, and the intense sexual musk of women that were sexually excited far beyond the level of arousal with which normal mortals could ever be familiar.

I had experienced erotic dreams before, but none had ever been even half as real to me as what I was experiencing at that time. The details of my surroundings were far too vivid, and everything seemed far too concrete for this to be part of any normal dream state. The old test of pinching myself to see if I was awake was impossible, since I could hardly move, but it wasn't necessary. I could feel every detail of everything around me, and I have never had a dream where the sounds, smells, and tactile senses were this acutely influenced by my surroundings. Aside from the bizarre and impossible situation, this seemed to be real in every possible sense of the word.

The crowd of women around me parted slightly to permit a strikingly beautiful woman with blonde hair and a lusciously curvy body enough room to stand above me, and I was mesmerized as she swayed her hips above me, sweat and sexual moisture dripping from her body onto mine as she undulated seductively in time to the music. Her hypnotic movements were beautiful and unhurried, and her motions reminded me of a strange and exotic cross between belly-dancing and some sort of erotic ballet. As she danced, her large breasts jiggled temptingly and beautifully, hinting at their full softness, and the beauty that rested between her soft white thighs promised pleasures that I craved with unspeakable intensity.

I looked up with longing at her perfect buttocks and the beautiful cleft at the juncture of her shapely legs as she swayed above me, but I couldn't move to touch her. Slowly, sensually, hypnotically, she moved her hips lower and lower as she danced to the pulsing drums, until the softness of her neat blonde pubic hair barely brushed and tickled my chest. Her muscular control was almost superhuman. My body demanded sexual release with an overwhelming, primal urgency that strained against my very sanity. I struggled against my invisible but unyielding bonds. Still, the gorgeous young woman was not done toying with me yet.

The beautiful stranger lowered herself even more. The beautiful pink petals of her womanhood kissed my chest, and she slid herself slowly along my abdomen and up to my sternum. I felt her sweet, warm vaginal moisture against my skin, so plentiful that a trail of it seeped from her and marked everywhere on my chest she touched. Her perfect ass felt warm and firm as she ground her pussy against my chest. With maddening patience, she slowly and rhythmically slid herself incrementally in unhurried undulations towards my face. Soon I could smell her delicious pussy, and inhale the delightful aroma of her arousal. If only she would bring her body closer so that I could lick and taste her! I have always loved orally pleasing a woman, but I had never desired it before so fervently as I did then. Or, alternately, if only she would slide back, mount my painfully hard cock, and grant us both sexual release through intercourse! But, instead, she ground herself against my chest in a gracefully controlled motion, and my arousal was reaching levels where I feared for my crumbling sanity if this were to continue. The girl beneath me was not half as graceful or controlled as the woman above me, and was rubbing herself wildly against my back as though her own need for sexual release were driving her every bit as insane with desire as my own need for sexual release was driving me. I certainly understood her frustration. If only I could roll over and allow myself to share blissful, glorious satisfaction with her, whoever she was!

Sliding herself further back to sit on my abdomen, the beautiful stranger leaned forward to kiss me deeply on the mouth. I tasted her sweet kisses and felt her soft breasts press firmly against my chest. Her perfect ass cheeks softly caressed the top of my penis between them, and her sweet womanhood rubbed against the muscles of my abdomen. I needed release desperately. She smiled at me with benign mockery, as though she were greatly amused by something that she knew and I didn't. She lifted her hips, letting her vaginal lips gently kiss the top of my cock. The brief contact was electrifying, but it was only for a moment before she slid her hips forward and away from my manhood.

It was with tremendous relief that I eventually felt the soft thighs of another woman straddle me behind the blonde stranger, and the head of my erect cock briefly brushed soft pubic hair and then touched moist, warm feminine flesh. I felt the lips of the pussy part around the head of my cock, admitting the tip of my manhood into the heat and moisture that lay behind them. Past the temptress that had cruelly tormented me with such unspeakable need, I saw wavy brown hair and had a brief feeling that there was something familiar about it.

The gorgeous blonde stranger cupped my head in her soft, warm hands and kissed me with a frightening, unnatural passion that spoke of madness and unspeakable need, and I felt her sweet, warm breath and soft blonde hair caress my face as the unseen woman behind her impaled herself on my cock, encasing my manhood in her blissful heat and moisture. My turgid member had grown so sensitive that I could feel every ecstatic detail, even the most minute of the small ridges inside of the delicious, wondrous, anonymous pussy that now stretched to accommodate my cock. As I continued to kiss the blonde woman, her hot wet tongue plundered my mouth and my own tongue responded in kind as our needy lips drank passion from one another. My hand, at last free to move, traveled down to her nether region, and I saw her smile I as she moved her hips to grant me easier access to the most intimate part of her lovely body. Her eyes grew wide as my fingers gained entrance to her warm haven. Thank heavens! At last I could move, and at last my cock was getting the attention it needed as the anonymous stranger began vigorously and passionately merging her sopping-wet sex with my hardness.

As my fingers worked inside of the beautiful blonde's wet pussy, the woman behind her rode me with passion and wild abandon, as though she were someone who had lusted after me for far too long, and could no longer be denied the lovemaking that she craved. The blonde stranger moved her head to kiss my face and my neck, and then slid gracefully off of my body and lay beside me, smiling at me with something like mirthful amusement and chuckling as though she had just played a joke on me that she found intensely amusing. With her no longer blocking my view, I looked up to see the brunette woman that had mercifully mounted me and granted me the promise of sexual release. To my horror, I immediately recognized that the woman who had for several minutes now been relishing the feeling of my throbbing penis buried deep within her silky depths was my own mother!

My mother's sweet, kind eyes were shining with wild, desperate passion as she rode me. The large, fleshy breasts from which I had nursed as an infant swayed as we fucked. My eyes traveled down my mother's stomach to the juncture of her thighs where my eyes confirmed what my penis had already told me. This was no illusion. I was indulging in the wickedly delectable sin of Oedipus Rex; I was actually fucking my own mother. She was beautiful, and I was horrified to feel my own desire for her swell and throb within my loins as her slippery birth canal gripped tightly around my steely-hard penis.

I was shocked by what was happening, but I was also far too aroused to stop. I needed release more desperately than I ever could have imagined possible; I felt certain that I would die without it. Above me, my beautiful, beloved mother bucked wildly, riding me like a pagan fertility goddess bent on conceiving a new world. The soft brown pubic hairs that adorned her luscious vulva ground hard against my pelvis. I looked between my mother's legs, watching my hardness engulfed within the same sweltering flesh from which I had been born. I could see the soft brown curls of my mother's vulva naturally forming a shape that vaguely resembled a heart, and the shiny pink lips of her glistening labia stretching tightly around the girth of my hard cock as she impaled herself upon me over and over again.

As my mother bounced on me, I could see her glistening fluids coating my manhood with a slippery sheen of forbidden moisture. Long ago, I had been born from that glorious pussy, and now I was returning and reveling in the wickedly taboo glory of the experience. My mother smiled sinfully as she ground her cervix against the head of my cock, and I was so sensitive that I could feel the tiny hole that marked the entrance to the very womb in which I had once resided. My mother looked down at me with fierce possessiveness as she claimed me as her son, her lover, and her mate. We fit together perfectly. My mother's familiar, beloved face was transformed and blazing with uncontrollable lust, and the large, pillow-soft breasts from which I had nursed in infancy bounced and jiggled obscenely as we fucked.

Countless female hands from all directions roamed our bodies as the unholy, incestuous union took place, as though the women around us were greedy to partake in the succulent wickedness of the blasphemous union. Fluids never intended to meet, the sexual nectar of a mother and her own son, were freely swapped as the head of my manhood ground hard against the smooth, slippery entrance to my own mother's womb. I felt her fingernails gently caress the top of my throbbing shaft as she massaged her clitoris, her tunnel becoming impossibly wetter while our sexual organs meshed together. She pounded herself down upon me, the wet sound of our coupling audible even above the crowd and the din of the insane pipes and drums. I couldn't help myself. My penis had never before been as hard as it now was as my mother forced me back deep into the core of her womanhood, and I rejoiced in every sensual detail of my immoral return to the warm, humid depths of the very womb where I had been created. Every sight, every, sound, every scent, every taste of what I was experiencing was forever burned into my memory.

I looked around me. My younger sister, Kim, a sprightly, innocent, 18-year-old pixie of a girl with short brown hair and sparkling eyes, was cuddling her petite young body against me to my left, her small warm hands traveling my chest as she humped her mound against my leg, the perfect brown nipples of her small, firm breasts massaging the side of my arm. One of her hands reached over, lovingly stroking my penis and our mother's vulva as she caressed the wet juncture where her brother and her mother were locked together in the most intimate of embraces. While it is impossible to know such things for certain, I felt positive that this was the first time that Kim had ever touched a penis. And it was her own brother's, even while I was involved in the act of fucking our own mother. Everything about this was wrong, forbidden, impossible! My innocent, virginal sister's wet, pink tongue traveled seductively along my neck and left a cool trail up the side of my face as I beheld my mother's body undulating and swaying above me in time to the drumbeats like some ancient pagan fertility goddess with my own mother's face. Glistening droplets of my mother's sweat were dripping from her breasts and sparkling like fiery jewels in the hellish torchlight.

My mother leaned down, her pendulous breasts crushing against my chest as she kissed me in a manner that no mother should ever kiss a son. My heart pounded in my chest like an industrial power-hammer, and my breathing was becoming increasingly rapid as I returned the kiss with equally scandalous passion. Breaking the kiss, she looked into my eyes.

"Look at me, sweetheart," my mother whispered before kissing me again. Her eyes met mine, and the expression on her face was almost tender as I felt her wet, scalding-hot insides continue to claim my manhood. "Look at your mother as we make love, and accept what we're doing together. I love you more than you could ever possibly know, and you need to know that what we are doing now is beautiful in every way. I need to feel you put your love deep inside of me. Cum inside of my pussy; Sweetheart; give your mother your sperm! Make me feel beautiful as you get me pregnant and make me a mother again! Let me know that my son will still want my pussy time and time again, even when my belly is swelling with our child!"

Higher and higher into ecstasy I climbed, and the drums and pipes played faster and faster as though fueled and driven by our ever-increasing spiral of arousal. My mother and I were rapidly approaching the point of no return, and still our genitals merged with wild, passionate need. My mother shrieked triumphantly as a steaming hot climax wracked her body with shuddering, quivering, convulsive ecstasy. Her soft, white, feminine thighs tightened around me like the jaws of a vice, and the velvet-soft walls of her wet, scalding-hot tunnel began to clench down in powerful spasmodic waves around my firm, throbbing manhood. She drenched me in her gloriously fertile maternal fluids as she gave herself over entirely to the ecstatic glory of her orgasm.

I could no longer prevent or even postpone the inevitable. My heart was pounding like race horse's, and my breath came in ragged gasps as every nerve in my trembling body fired at once. My thoughts went blank as my brain was deliciously electrocuted by my own powerful orgasm. My body was flooded with far more pleasure than any human being was ever wired to experience, so much pleasure that it was almost painful to feel it all at once, as my own climax fertilized my mother's ripe body. My penis was pressing hard and sealing against the firm, slippery, muscular opening of my mother's cervix. I felt defeat and the loss of so much more than sperm as jet after hot liquid jet of my potent seed gushed deeply into her hot, wet depths, defiling her eager maternal womb with her own son's semen. Still she continued in her climax, her beautiful body shuddering and undulating above me as the slippery walls of her pussy fluttered against the hardness of the spurting member that I continued to thrust deep into her innermost depths. I reveled in the knowledge that I was impregnating my own mother, even while experiencing shock and horror that I could revel in the pleasure of such an intensely depraved act.

After the slippery wet flesh of my mother's heavenly vagina had milked me of every drop of potent semen that my body could provide, she kissed me tenderly and lovingly on my lips. As I returned the kiss, our mouths opened and our wet lips and tongues slowly mated. I was still buried deep within her pussy as she crushed her entire body against mine. Any barriers or taboos between us had melted like snow on a hot summer's day. I knew that my mother and I would be repeating this act, even as she had said while we were making love. Slowly, she raised her hips, sliding the sinful pussy that was now dripping with our mingled fluids from my still-hard cock. The act was almost painful for me.

My mother kissed me a final time and slid her slick, sweaty body from on top of me. The hard brown nipples of her hot, perspiration-drenched breasts dragged lewdly across my chest as the beautiful stranger on my right side- I now realized that my fingers were still deep inside of her body and she was just finishing an orgasm of her own while witnessing the incestuous act- stood up and moved away from us, making room for my mother to cuddle almost sweetly against my side.

My mother stared almost tenderly into my eyes as my sweet, virginal young sister climbed on top of me. I couldn't get up, or even move. This was going to happen, and I couldn't avoid it any more than I could have stopped what I had just done with my mother.

"It's my turn now, brother," my delicate young sister whispered hotly into my ear.

"Mom, Kim's still a virgin!" I protested.

"Only for a few more seconds," my mother replied in a sardonically soothing tone as she reached over and grasped my cock, which was still slippery and literally dripping with the sexual fluids of our own unholy union. Impossibly, even after the greatest orgasm of my life, my erection was still undiminished in hardness, and my body was already insistently demanding more sex. Now, with the same hands with which my mother had held us, calmed us, and fed us as children, my mother now placed the head of my cock at the opening of her own daughter's still-virginal slit. I could see and feel myself pressed into the warm, yielding softness of my sister's innocent vulva, and my heart leapt into my throat.

Other anonymous women- and I now prayed that they would remain anonymous- pressed their warm and receptive feminine flesh against my vulnerable body from every direction. Someone I could not see was now grinding her clitoris against my shin, and while I could not see her face I felt the deliciously soft wetness of her slit and the supple cushions of her womanly ass, and I knew that I desired her. She felt amazing. Sitting on the grass near my head, I recognized my Aunt Cindy, who was still remarkably attractive despite her age. Her chest was heaving, her eyes half shut, her shapely legs spread and her hand working feverishly between them as she watched her nephew and her sister frantically rutting together so close that she could have reached out and touched us with her fingers which were glistening with slickness from her own feminine juices. I couldn't see any more faces in the kaleidoscope of human flesh that whirled around me, and I feared who else I might recognize if I could.

I looked down at my sweet younger sister's nude body as she straddled me. Like my mother, she was beautiful, her body athletic and well-proportioned. I had never seen her naked before, at least since we were too young to think anything of it, and I was horrified by my body's eagerness to complete the wicked act that was now all but certain to occur. What I had just done with my mother had felt far too wonderful for words to possibly express it. Even so, I could not defile my virginal sister's body.

"Kim," I pleaded even as I felt my body pressing up against her as though acting of its own accord, "You don't have to do this! I don't want to take your virginity! For the love of God, what has gotten into you?" Even as I spoke, my body betrayed me as my hips pressed upwards into the warm softness between her legs. My sister smiled at me as the purple head of my rock-hard manhood began to slowly press against her impenetrably tight orifice.

Kim looked into my eyes, her face glowing in the torchlight. Her pupils were dilated with adrenaline and her eyes wild with need and reflecting fire from the torches. "So, brother," she said, emphasizing my relationship to her as though the word tasted delicious on her tongue, "You say that you don't want my virginity, but I haven't moved. You're the one pressing up against my pussy. Am I supposed to believe your words or your actions? Tell me that you don't want this," she said as she ground her delightful vagina against me, "and I'll stop." She kissed me wickedly and incestuously as she pressed her pussy down harder against me, and I could feel the sacred membrane of her innocence begin straining against my cockhead.

With a groan, I pushed back, feeling my cock burrow a tiny bit deeper into her. My need boiled within my veins like lava. I needed my sister's virginity like a drowning man needs oxygen, and my lust was quickly drowning out my capacity for rational thought.

My sister smiled, rubbing her wet pussy against my penis as the last vestiges of my self control disintegrated. "That's what I thought. So, do you want to take my virginity? Do you want to fuck your sister without any protection and cum inside of her?"

My heart sank in despair as my own voice responded, "Yes."

The pressure between my manhood and the most sacred and intimate parts of my sister's delicate young body suddenly increased. She was soaking wet, and my penis was still lubricated from forbidden sex with our mother. But Kim was so tight that I still hadn't managed to breach her innocent pussy. Her soft, full lips pressed hard against my own in a scandalous, wicked, open-mouthed lover's kiss, which I returned and loved every second of it. I tasted the sweetness of my sister's saliva, her tongue wrestling wetly with my own.

She pulled away, and I saw my sweet, familiar little sister's face staring down at me, blazing with lust and madness as her eyes locked upon my owns. "Prepare to feel my virginity poured out upon you. Make me a woman, brother." Her words burned into my brain and her eyes smoldered with feverish madness as she forced her painfully tight vagina down upon my cock, a cock that was still slick with the natural lubrication from the wicked union of her own brother and her mother. I slid partly into her sopping wet tunnel. I heard her emit a sharp gasp, and I felt the barrier that had guarded her maidenhood for 18 years tear as she relentlessly and forcefully impaled herself on me with a need that overruled any level of discomfort. It felt as though her body were splitting in half around my cock, and she arched her back and shrieked in something that could have been any possible combination of joy, pain, triumph, or unbridled sexual ecstasy as she continued forcing her body relentlessly downward onto mine.

My manhood was soon entirely gripped within the heat and moisture of my sister's body, her virginal tunnel tighter than a clenched fist around my cock. For long moments she sat frozen above me, the full length of my penis firmly sheathed inside of her delicate young reproductive tract. She looked beautiful as she sat above me, her thighs spread beside my hips and her back arched, her small, firm breasts proudly thrust forward. My sister was no longer a virgin, and it was my fault.

She leaned over, and again, Kim's tongue softly caressed my neck. Looking over her shoulder, I had a brief glimpse of the woman who was grinding herself against my leg, and recognized my favorite cousin, Heather. Older and sweeter than her sister, Sarah, Heather had been my close friend since birth. She was sweet, restrained, and most definitely not someone that would ever take part in a blasphemous rite like this under any circumstances. But here she was nonetheless, and I had no doubt that it was only a matter of time before she replaced the leg she was humping with my hard cock. I had always loved Heather, but had never looked at her sexually before, and my heart ached with the thought of the innocent relationship that might be changed forever if I were to let Heather mount me. Over and over again I assured myself that this was only a dream. But it certainly did not feel like one.

Those thoughts were immediately obscured as Kim finished planting a decadently wet kiss on my neck, then moved her face to mine and she kissed me deeply and passionately on the mouth. I was unable to stop myself from returning the kiss; I needed her as desperately as she needed me. Our tongues writhed together, mimicking the similar union of of our drenched sexual organs. I felt my sister's soft breath against my sweaty skin as she whispered fiercely, "Yesssss! You have made me a woman, now make me the mother of your child!" Her eyes blazed with wild intensity as I looked into the face of my sweet younger sister. Even the knowledge that something had completely transformed my dear little sister with an infusion of unspeakable lust was not sufficient to save me from betrayal by my own body. I cried out in alarm as I erupted yet again in a powerful orgasm, knowing that I had just conceived a child with my own mother, and I was now about to become a father to my own sister's baby.

As my sister and I continued to cum together, our kisses became animalistic, deep, sloppy, and uncontrolled as her sweet vagina spasmed around my cock, milking me of far more sperm-rich semen than I would normally even be able to produce in a week. For several minutes my body and hers writhed together, struggling to force my ejaculating penis as deep into her receptive depths as possible.

My sister's nubile young body was demanding sperm to fill her fertile young womb and fallopian tubes, and my body was insistent upon claiming the privilege of fertilizing the ripe fruit of my own sister's ovaries. Neither of our bodies were denied the fulfillment of their needs. When we were finally spent, Kim slid herself slowly off of my cock. Semen shot through with streaks of her sacred virginal blood slowly leaked from the no-longer-innocent orifice that in nine months would be giving birth to the natural product of an unnatural union between two siblings. I felt another woman move into position, and I didn't have to look to know that it was my childhood friend and companion, Heather, that was about to forever change a lifetime of happy, innocent memories with an act of incestuous lust. Again I reminded myself that, although I was certain that this was by far the most realistic dream that I had ever experienced, this had to be a dream. None of this was real. It couldn't be.

My sister slid out of the way, and now I found myself with my mother cuddled against my right side, my sister cuddled against my left side, and someone I couldn't see writhing against my back directly beneath me. The woman beneath me was desperately grinding her drenched vulva against my back in a futile effort to achieve sexual satisfaction. She had been there the whole time, although I had been so distracted that I had hardly noticed her, and her sexual frustration was a palpable thing. Although I could move almost freely once again, it was as though some invisible but irresistible force were physically preventing me from being able to turn my head to see who the girl underneath me was.

Looking to my left, I saw my beautiful sister lying against me, her face glowing with satisfaction and my seed mingled with a hint of her virginal blood drooling from her freshly deflowered pussy. For the first time, I noticed a tattoo on her left hip. It was a small, stylized heart with the words "Love is Forever" written around it in flowing script, and I felt grateful for the confirmation that this wasn't actually happening. I had seen Kim in a swimsuit just a few months ago. She had no tattoos, and surely she would have mentioned it to me if she had gotten one. We had always been close.

I looked down at Heather, seeing her familiar, round, friendly face, her long, straight blonde hair, and her beautiful smile. Her sky-blue eyes regarded me lovingly from behind the familiar prescription glasses that constituted the only thing she was currently wearing. Sweet, quiet, and bookish, with a wicked sense of humor that only reveals itself to those that she knows well, Heather has always been my closest confidant and my favorite family member. I had honestly never thought of her sexually before tonight, and I had never before seen her wearing any less than a conservative, one-piece swimsuit.

My gaze traveled down from Heather's familiar, beloved face to her chest. She was pleasantly plump, her pale, chubby body sporting large, fleshy breasts that might have sagged slightly more than those of most girls our age, but on Heather that characteristic only seemed cute and endearing. It was part of someone I had always loved, and I was enticed by the exotic newness of seeing my cousin's breasts. I noted the large, pink, puffy nipples and aureolas that adorned her succulent breasts, and the smooth, soft roundness of her belly. Then my gaze finally dared to travel downwards to her wide, womanly hips, the junction of Heather's smooth white thighs, and the soft, heart-shaped nest of thick, dark-blonde curls that covered her most intimate parts. Her ass was facing away from me, but for the first time in my life I contemplated the healthy, perfectly-shaped roundness of her butt. I had never before seen my cousin as a sexual being, or contemplated the soft fullness of her beautiful womanly curves and ample femininity. Seeing her as I did now, I wondered why I had never noticed her in that way before. Everything about Heather seemed in one sense endearingly and charmingly familiar, but the sultry nakedness of her beautifully rubinesque body so close to mine filled me with excitement and need.

"I've always thought that the two of you would make an adorable couple," my Aunt Cindy breathed to us as she continued to play with herself. Her legs were shaking, and her pretty face was drawn and tight with barely-controlled lust. She was restraining herself from climbing on top of me only for the sake of her daughter. She looked at Heather. "Do it, Sweety," she said to her daughter in an urgent whisper. "Breed with your cousin. You've always wanted him. He's yours now. Please, make beautiful grandchildren for me." Taking my penis in a warm, soft hand that was still wet from rubbing her own sodden vagina, Aunt Cindy placed the head of my cock against her daughter's moist opening.

Heather looked into my eyes as she allowed her aroused, engorged vaginal lips to gently kiss the head of my penis. She moved slowly, as though savoring the moment that she claimed something that she had always wanted. I felt the heat and moisture radiating from my beloved cousin's fertile core as, for the first time, I breached the most intimate part of her body.

My heart pounded as though it would explode in my chest. Still, my beautiful cousin held her ample hips high, so that only her outer lips were spread by the throbbing flesh of my engorged cock head. Looking down at me, Heather smiled at me lovingly. I couldn't resist returning the smile; the silliness and impossibility of our situation was immediately amusing to us both. We both knew that this couldn't be happening. This was impossible; our mothers would never act like this. It was as though we were both aware that we were sharing an impossibly vivid dream, but we had always cared deeply for one another and were determined to enjoy it while it lasted. Both of us wanted to enjoy the secret embrace that was available to us in this dream where we could have what we wanted with no repercussions or consequences, and no one would ever know. We wouldn't even have to risk confessing our forbidden lust to each other.

My own mother, so recently fertilized from making love to me, reached out with a trembling hand and reverently caressed my cock, running her hand up to stroke Heather's beautiful opening, and then lingering at the place where my cousin and I were joined by only the slightest bit of penetration. Heather gasped quietly as she allowed her body to slide down less than a centimeter, still taking only about half of the head of my cock inside of her. She was so wet that she could have claimed my full length easily with a single motion, but she didn't. Heather loved me and needed the reassurance that I needed her as badly as she needed me, and both of us wanted this moment to last forever.

As my mother lovingly stroked the genitals of her son and her niece, she looked at me and smiled. "You're ready for this. Now, let your cousin show you how much she has always cared for you."

I smiled at my beloved cousin. "I love you, Heather. Please give yourself to me. This is just a dream, right? It's totally safe."

She kissed me tenderly, still keeping just the tip of my penis inside of her. "I never thought I could have this," she said with a voice choked with emotion. She sounded as though she might cry. "This dream just feels so real. It's hard to believe that I'll wake up tomorrow feeling like I've gotten to make love to you, and you won't know that anything has happened."

She thought that this was her dream? Why would I be dreaming that? "I'll never forget anything about what we're about to do, Heather. I promise. Please, give yourself to me and let me give myself to you."

Heather didn't claim my body as suddenly or forcefully as my mother and sister had. Instead, she lowered herself upon me slowly, as though intent on savoring every minute detail of the experience, feeling herself being penetrated by a beloved friend that she had never thought she could have as a lover. Tenderly, with love and compassion in her eyes, she leaned down and kissed me softly on the lips. She still gently held the very tip of my hardness inside of herself, as though she wanted to make the moment that I first penetrated her, the instant that we first gained sexual knowledge of our beloved cousin, last forever. Her fleshy breasts, as soft as clouds, dragged hard nipples across my chest.

Heather reached her soft white arms around me and embraced me lovingly. Planting a soft, almost chaste kiss upon my lips, she whispered the words, "I have always loved you." Then her eyes closed halfway and she sighed sweetly as she began slowly lowering her pelvis upon me. Heat and moisture encased my rampant member until I was entirely sheathed inside the moist depths of my beloved cousin's fleshy warmth. Her pure, sweet, sexual fluids washed over my cock, bathing it in a steamy, sacred baptism of liquid love. I felt the tip of my penis rub against her cervix as we slowly mated, and contemplated the fact that I was actually touching the entrance to the sacred chamber where the fruit of our love would implant and grow.

Aunt Cindy, Heather's mother, moved over and took my sister's place lying by our side, one of her hands lovingly caressing the joined bodies of her daughter and her nephew, the other hand moving between her legs in time to the motions that Heather and I were making as though she wished that she could feel what her daughter was experiencing. Aunt Cindy wanted to be as close as she could to her daughter and her nephew as we engaged in this beautiful and sacred, if taboo, act. She wanted to be part of the act that would create new life within her daughter, and make her a grandmother. On our other side, my own mother was gently stroking Heather's body and my own as she rubbed her sopping pussy. She, like her sister, was about to become a grandmother. Even as Heather and I were mating, deep within my mother, one lucky sperm was fertilizing a ripe egg within her own fallopian tubes. The sexual ecstasy of my union with Heather combined with the lifetime of love and friendship that my cousin and I had always shared, and brought us both to unbearable heights of passion and ecstasy. I knew that it was only a short matter of time before our union reached its natural culmination in a white-hot explosion of pure love and sexual energy.

Our shared climax was like a great dam that burst, and both my cousin and I felt ourselves being willingly swept away by the raw power that was unleashed within our bodies. Heather's body and my own felt transported by an impossible pinnacle of rapturous ecstasy; we felt sexual fulfillment with such immense force that it transcended my entire concept of the word "orgasm". Neither of us were aware of anything else. Our eyes were clenched shut, and her mouth opened wide in a gasping, uninhibited cry of unbridled pleasure and joy. Our bodies quivered and shook, and we embraced each other with all of our trembling strength as I poured myself deep into my beloved cousin's fertile depths and her body drank my offering greedily as her vagina clenched powerfully and rhythmically around my swollen cock. Two more arms belonging to my mother and Aunt Cindy were wrapped tightly around us, and both of them cried out with wild, joyous triumph as all four of us experienced earth- shatteringly powerful orgasms, all at the exact same moment. None of our lives could ever be the same again after experiencing something so perfect and beautiful together.

It was almost 7:00 when I awoke in a panic, my head swimming with the heady aftereffects of such a bizarre dream. I was lucky that I had packed for the trip the night before, because in an unprecedented stroke of bad luck both of my alarm clocks had somehow failed me. I was already supposed to be at Steve and Frank's house helping to load gear, and in just a few moments they were likely to be leaving without me. Grabbing my cellphone and tossing the charger into a side pouch of my rucksack, I tried calling Diana's cellphone.

Diana, or Diane as we sometimes call her, is a close friend of mine, and together she and I are the unofficial leaders of the paranormal research club. We semi-jokingly compare our roles to the positions of a platoon leader and a platoon sergeant, although both of us claimed that we were the NCO and jokingly accused the other of fulfilling the role of a clueless lieutenant. We were, in reality, normally both very competent and reliable individuals. I cursed my luck. Diana's phone was busy, and my call went directly to voice mail.

I skipped breakfast, hurriedly brushed my teeth, threw my rucksack in my car. While driving, although I knew that it wasn't safe, I tried calling Steve's cellphone, then Frank's. Neither of them answered. I tried Diana's phone again, and it was still busy.

Most policemen will tolerate someone driving up to five miles an hour over the speed limit, and I did so all the way over to Steve and Frank's house. I still didn't manage to get there until 7:30. The paranormal research club, unlike most organizations of the sort, usually left on time and being late often meant being left behind. Especially if you showed up an hour later than you were supposed to, and thirty minutes after the group was scheduled to leave like I was today. Many of the sites we research involve either a limited time period of access to a privately owned site that is often someone's home, or they involve meeting the property's owners at a prearranged time and it's rude and unprofessional for us to be late. Paranormal researchers get enough of a bad rap among the general public that we are very careful not to do anything to appear unprofessional or inconsiderate, especially towards someone that has kindly allowed us access to a reputedly haunted site. And today, with a trip of well over 13 hours ahead of us that would already have us awakening Erin's parents at midnight with our arrival, the club would have certainly wanted to leave on schedule.

I wondered briefly why Diane or someone else hadn't called me like they normally would have, but then I realized that if I had somehow slept through two alarms going off, then I probably would have slept right through my phone ringing as well. How had this happened? I'm usually a very light sleeper. The shame of potentially disappointing my friends burned in my face as I drove.

I pulled into the gravel driveway, stirring up a cloud of gray dust and startling a large flock of boisterous black birds that had congregated around a crooked old pecan tree in the front lawn. There were only two other cars in the driveway aside from those that belonged to Steve and Frank. The battered white van was still parked in its customary place beneath a gnarled old oak tree, so I knew with some relief that I hadn't missed the trip. I recognized one of the parked cars as Erin's. The other car belonged to Diana.

Diana was tall, with short black hair and piercing sapphire-blue eyes. She was one of those people that looked a bit chubby at first glance, but she moved with a grace that spoke of natural strength and athleticism that stemmed from a lifetime of martial arts training and other competitive sports. Most of her extra mass was truly muscle, not fat. Her sturdy limbs had earned her a softball scholarship for her first two years of college before she had injured her shoulder in a motorcycle accident and had to stop playing. She was a staff sergeant in a local National Guard military police unit, and had served tours in both Iraq and Afghanistan. As a fellow veteran of those wars, I was one of the few friends that she would discuss them with, but neither of us liked the topic and we usually tried to avoid it unless one or both of us was extremely drunk. Yes, we have both had to shoot and kill people. I'm not trying to be rude or unfriendly, but neither of us wish to discuss it with anyone.

Twice a week, when she could spare the time, Diana served as an assistant instructor at a local martial arts school that taught traditional aikido, a Japanese martial art that focuses on throwing and joint locks. Despite the fact that she talked less than most girls her age and she spoke with a maturity and an air of authority that marked her as a natural leader, she was friendly, well-liked, and had numerous tasteful but brilliantly executed tattoos that she had drawn herself. I had never gotten to see all of them, which I regarded as very unfortunate. Some of Diana's tattoos were, if I were to believe her playful hints, in some very interesting locations on her body. Like me, Diana didn't like crowds or enjoy socializing much, and I think that the paranormal research club gave her a good social outlet that didn't make her feel too uncomfortable or demand excessive interaction with people that she didn't know well. Even when we weren't ghost hunting, it wasn't unusual for Diana or I to be spending time together. We were always over at each others' house for one reason or another, and we meant the world to each other. But, despite the fact that some people thought we were dating, or thought that we should start dating, our close friendship combined with the fact that both she and I had a tendency towards romantic relationships that ended disastrously had long ago caused us to agree to never risk our friendship by becoming romantically entangled together.

I parked my car, shouldered my rucksack, and jogged across the gravel driveway towards the battered wooden door that served as the side entrance to Steve and Frank's house. On the way, I glanced through the back windows of the van, and noticed that it hadn't yet even been loaded with suitcases or gear. I knocked as I pressed through the battered white-painted wooden door with its loose old doorknob, and I strode into the familiar old farmhouse kitchen which served as our unofficial meeting room and headquarters. On the ancient, cracked, and stained black-and-white tiled floor stood a large old-fashioned kitchen table, made of well-worn oak and suitable for dinner with a huge 19th century farming family. Erin and Diana were sitting at the table quietly sipping coffee. While I was relieved that there would still be time for my morning caffeine kick, I immediately picked up on the aura of disappointment that emanated from the two young ladies.

"Sorry I'm late. Would you believe that neither of my two alarm clocks went off? So, where is everyone?" I asked Erin and Diana as I dropped my rucksack in a corner beside Erin's suitcase and Diana's duffel bag.

Erin stared at her cold coffee in glum silence, and made small clinking sounds as she absently stirred it with a spoon. I hadn't seen her look that sad since her dog had died the previous summer.

Diana smiled tightly as she looked up at me. "Thanks for coming, John, but we're everyone. Steve and Frank tried the new Mexican place over by the park last night, and now they're both sick with food poisoning. Mark woke up this morning with his basement flooded from a broken water pipe. I would have called you earlier, but he was pretty upset and I've been on the phone with him. Apparently a lot of his stuff has been ruined, including most of his books and art supplies, and most of his thesis project has been destroyed. I finally got off the phone with him and I was just about to call you to tell you not to bother coming when we looked out the window and saw your car approaching down the road. Sorry, but I don't think we'll be able to do it this year."

Erin sighed, but didn't respond. She was graduating in a few months, and moving away to take a job back in Vermont. This was likely to be the last chance she would have to coordinate an investigation at her parents' church. She had really been looking forward to this, and she really hated to disappoint her parents. More than once she had talked about how much our willingness to research the old church and document what we found there would mean to her father.

"Hey, how about this: we can put off leaving until tomorrow so we can spend today seeing if we can scrape together anyone to fill the empty slots, then head up there a day late?" I offered. "For now, how about breakfast at that little hole-in-the-wall mom- and-pop place that Erin likes over by Main street? I don't know about you two, but I skipped breakfast this morning."

Diana smiled at me. "That's a great thought, but I don't know if we'll have enough time for a good investigation if we loose a day. Mark has to stick around until his landlord can get a plumber out to his place, and even then he said that he has to re-do most of his thesis project on top of getting everything squared away with his renter's insurance. And based on the noises that I've heard come out of the bathroom this morning, I don't know if Steve and Frank are going to be up to a long car trip for a good long while. Most of the other regular members either have to work or are out of town for Spring Break. You know how much her Dad sounds like he cares about this; I would hate to disappoint him with half-assed work. If Erin's parents are going to pay for us to drive that gas-guzzling behemoth halfway across the country and then take care of us all while we're there, we owe them a good, professional-quality investigation. So, barring a miracle, the trip isn't happening." She looked at Erin. "So, how does some nice artery-clogging breakfast food sound? Come on, it will cheer you up."

Erin smiled at her friends and smiled thinly. "Sure! Let's go."

We took Diana's car over to the restaurant, and sat in our customary booth in the back. Feeling gallant, I offered to pay for the two ladies.

"Hey, John!" cried a familiar voice from across the room.

I looked over to a table by the window, and saw my sister, Kim, sitting with my cousins Heather and Sarah. They had just been served breakfast, and looked like they were all just sitting down to eat. Across the table from them was my mother, Alice. She had met my friends in the club before, and she smiled and waved at us.

While etiquette would normally require that we join them, since they were here first and already had their food, the booth where we were sitting was more than spacious enough to accommodate 7 people if my mother sat at a chair on the end of the table, and the table that my family sat at would barely accommodate the four trays that already crowded it.

"Hey, y'all! Why don't you come over and join us?" I offered. I felt a bit awkward facing my relatives after such a vivid, realistic dream about them the previous night, but I determined to simply get over it. It was just a dream, right?

"So why aren't you guys halfway to Vermont by now? I thought that you were pretty excited to be doing this." My mother asked the group as she approached us. Maybe it was my imagination, but were my mother and Kim avoiding eye contact with me? Heather looked happier and healthier than normal, and she smiled me with even more than her usual warmth. Sarah, the only one of the four that I hadn't seen in my dream, leered at me like a tiger eying a steak. Kim seemed to be walking in a way that was almost imperceptibly unusual. I quickly put the thought of her loosing her virginity in last night's dream out of my mind.

Erin smiled sadly and answered for the group of us. "It clearly just wasn't meant to be. We're three people short, and that means that we don't have enough people to do a good job investigating my dad's church."

Kim looked at me, then back to Erin. Kim had occasionally tagged along on our ghost-hunting excursions, and she and Erin had developed a pretty close friendship on their own over the last few years. "I was just over there talking to my Mom and cousins about this awesome trip that John was going to get to go on, and that I didn't get to go because you already had everyone you needed! If I can go, count me in! Not to mention, Heather and Sarah thought it sounded awesome. I could totally throw my stuff in a bag and be ready to go in an hour!" Kim glanced at Heather and Sarah. "If you come, we'll have just as many people as they were originally planning to have, and I can explain everything you need to know about what to do on the way there. Come on! You were both just talking about how you didn't have any major plans for Spring Break, and this is going to be awesome!"

Sarah was short and slender, with a cute pixie-cut that was somewhere between blonde and light brown, tanned skin, and adorable little freckles on her nose and cheeks. Upon hearing Kim's offer, she immediately squealed an excited "Hell yeah!" and then looked at her sister, Heather, expectantly.

After the dream last night, I saw Heather differently than I previously had. She really was a very pretty woman, and her pale complexion and light blond hair all made her even more beautiful in my eyes. My eyes traveled down, admiring the swells of her large breasts and her wide, feminine hips. I briefly reminisced about how she had looked and felt in my dream from the previous night as I looked admiringly at her face, remembering how it had felt to kiss her, to touch her, and to make love to her. I looked at her and felt my breathing quicken. I could almost feel myself inside of her again. Suddenly, I realized that I was checking out my cousin, and she was looking at me intently. My eyes met hers, and, for a long moment, Heather met my gaze. Then she blushed a deep crimson then shyly averted the sky-blue eyes that peeked out from behind her thick glasses.

While Heather didn't usually volunteer for this sort of crazy adventure, she was the sort of person that never liked to disappoint anyone. If her sister and cousins needed her for this, then she was going to Vermont. Still, she glanced at my mother before making a decision.

My mother, Alice, smiled sweetly at Heather. "You run on with your sister and cousin. I love you all, but from what John and Kim have been saying this sounds like you're going to have a lot of fun, and, frankly I think it will be nice to have the house to myself for a few days!"

"I love you too, Mom!" Kim said with playfully feigned rejection.

Heather smiled and her sweet round face lit up as she displayed a pretty row of clean, white, evenly spaced teeth. "I'm in." She looked at me, as though looking forward to spending time together, then she looked at my mother, Alice. "Are you sure you won't be lonely until Mom gets back from that business trip to Seattle?"

My mother looked at her with a sweet smile. "I'm sure. It will be nice to get caught up on my writing. As a matter of fact, if you guys come back with some good scary experiences, tell me about them and they might give me some ideas for my next book!" She winked at us, giving the impression that she was joking. But despite being a moderately successful author that would never lack for money due to the success of her first several books, she had been having a hard time producing the same quality of material since my father had died. He had been a healthy 50-year-old man with a body that most men would have envied when they were 20. He had been out running for exercise early in the morning before work when a drunk driver, who had only then been leaving the bar, swerved across the road and struck my father from behind despite the bright yellow reflective vest that Dad always wore when running before it was light. Shortly after the tragedy, we had moved here to be closer to my maternal Aunt Cindy and her daughters. When Aunt Cindy's husband left her, they had moved into our large house with us while the courts got everything settled from the divorce, and then they just stayed on as permanent roommates. I half-jokingly complained that I was surrounded by an unhealthy level of estrogen, but it was still nice to have so much family around.

I briefly considered what it would mean for Kim, Heather, and Sarah to tag along on this investigation. Kim had been on a few of our excursions, but nothing quite like this before. This was definitely not an ideal investigation to take beginners on, both because Erin's family was counting on a professional investigation and because the particulars of what Erin and her family had told us about the site sounded like this was a very active intelligent haunting that might be very frightening even for seasoned investigators, and it might possibly even be dangerous for beginners. Our discussions with Professor Morrison had us very interested in the site, but also a bit frightened of it. We couldn't categorize the haunting except to say that there were most definitely several very active intelligent entities involved, but there were also several very unusual features of this haunting that made it almost impossible to categorize.

My family sounded excited about coming, and I hated to disappoint them. I told myself that everything would probably be fine if we put each less experienced person with a more experienced person, and it sounded like my family had already made the decision to come with us anyway. To forbid them from coming would probably disappoint everyone here, and hauntings that are physically dangerous to people are rare enough that I could probably get away with taking a chance on a site just this once. After all, Erin and her family were all just fine and they lived there, right?

Sarah got up from the table and walked towards the restroom, still smiling. "Be right back. I'm so excited that we're going to get to go!" She giggled excitedly and did a little dance as she walked to the door into the ladies' room.

"So the three of you can come? Great!" Diana beamed towards Kim. "After we eat, why don't you three go home, pack your bags, and then meet us at Steve and Frank's house as soon as you can get ready! Kim, you know how to get there, right? Good! Be sure to pack sleeping bags, since we'll be camping tonight on the way there. Also, pack warmer clothes than you usually would for this time of year, and a small flashlight or two if you've got one. Preferably something that runs off of double or triple A batteries, and if not then bring lots of extra batteries to make sure you don't run out. If you need sleeping bags, flashlights, or anything else, tell us and we'll bring extras."

The directions we had printed off from the internet said that the trip to the parsonage where Erin's parents' lived, and the haunted church directly beside it, would be about thirteen and a half hours away from our hometown. That said, the internet doesn't have to stop to eat, use the restroom, or refill the constantly draining gas tank. The big van was as comfortable as a large boat on the ocean, gently creaking and rocking as it sped down the interstate. We were getting a late start, so Diana had wisely decided to make the trip over the course of the next two days and get into Erin's parents' place at a reasonable hour tomorrow. That way there would be plenty of time for Erin and her family to give us a tour of the place, point out areas where things frequently happened and tell us what to expect, and we would have time to set up our equipment before it got dark. Erin's father had amused us all with his insistence upon being present for the walk-through. As we headed down the road, Diana at the wheel and Erin in the front passenger seat, Erin explained to Kim, Heather, and Sarah what the rest of us already knew about the old church where her father preached.

"The original structure that stood where my father's church now sits was a Roman Catholic church that was built by the French some time about 1743. Like a lot of churches in the area at that time, it was also one of the sturdier log buildings in town, and it doubled as something like a little fort when the community was threatened. During the French and Indian War, a company of British Rangers attacked the settlement while on their way to raid a larger French trading post to the north. When the French settlers barricaded themselves in the church, the British left a squad of their best riflemen behind to watch the church and ensure that nobody escaped alive to warn the trading post that British troops were coming. For the next two days the British riflemen watched the place like hawks, and their snipers picked off anyone that dared to show themselves. A total of five men and two women are said to have been killed in or near the church by the British. The French couldn't leave the church, so they chose to bury their dead beneath its earthen floor. On the third day, the main body of the British returned through the town laden with scalps and trade goods they had recovered from the trading post. The riflemen rejoined the main body, and they disappeared into the forest as a unit."

"At the end of the French and Indian War, the land was ceded to Great Britain. The small church became Anglican, and it's still Episcopalian to this day. In 1782, the original structure was badly damaged during a skirmish between American patriots and British loyalists. Remembering the fate of the Frenchmen that had died defending the church, the Americans buried the dead Tories beneath what had been the earthen floor of the humble old church, disturbing the bones of several long-dead French settlers in the process. And so the church lay desecrated and in disrepair for over thirty years. In 1813, immediately following the War of 1812, the church was rebuilt out of locally made bricks by a wealthy local gentleman. I suppose, more realistically, it was rebuilt by his slaves. When constructing what is currently the basement of the church, the bones of the Frenchmen and

British loyalists were, of necessity, disinterred. Disdain for the British was running high at that time, and the locals refused to have the bones buried in the same churchyard where their friends and family lay. The first pastor of the rebuilt church was afraid that burying the bones outside of the graveyard would result in the graves being desecrated by angry locals, so remembering the charnel houses of old Europe, he consolidated the bones into neat piles in a small room in the back of the basement. He was an elderly veteran of the French and Indian War and the Revolution, and while he apparently approved of his old enemies' bones being artfully arranged behind closed doors as a sufficiently respectful alternative to traditional burial, he adamantly refused to ever go into the basement himself, and he would not even go near the church at night. The pages of his diary that have survived are the first written documents that imply that the church might have been haunted."

Kim smiled. "So, tell me if I've got this right: we've got lots of people dying suddenly and violently in the prime of their lives, the French wanted to warn their countrymen about the British attack so you have people that died with unfinished business, you've got desecrated graves... wow! Any one of these things can make a place haunted, right? Hey, when John was telling me about this place, he was saying that there was some priest who killed himself in the church protecting buried treasure?"

Erin smiled back at her, but the smile seemed forced, as though it were more of a mask to hide something else than a reflection of real happiness. "There are a lot of stories about that old place, and I've seldom researched any of them that didn't turn out to be based on truth.

You see, during the mid 1700s, an Anglican bishop brought a large chest full of valuables from St. Bride's and other churches in London over to decorate the fledgeling churches here in the colonies. His writings seem to indicate that he thought that somehow prettier churches would have a civilizing effect on the unruly, rough-and-ready colonists. Most of what he brought ended up at King's Chapel in Boston, which had been founded during the 1600's. That church is still standing, by the way, but it's Unitarian now. Anyway, when the Revolution began, all property of the crown was considered fair game for confiscation by the United States in order to support their own underfunded war effort, and property of the Anglican church was sometimes regarded as something of a gray area depending on how underfunded the local Patriots were at the moment. But some members of the Anglican clergy viewed the Revolution as treason and refused to support it. The valuables were discreetly smuggled out of Boston shortly after the Boston Massacre, when it became apparent that there would be trouble. Thinking that an inconspicuous hiding place in a more remote location would make the treasure as difficult to find as possible, as well as easier for a small force of British troops to recover without running into massed resistance, the treasure was smuggled into Vermont and is reputed to be hidden somewhere near my father's church. When an American colonel showed up at the church demanding to know the location of the treasure in order to pay his bedraggled, half-starved battalion of American infantrymen, the crazed local priest told him that he would rather go to the Devil than see His

Majesty's gold fall into the hands of the Patriots. Then, right in the middle of the church in front of the horrified soldiers, he pulled a horse pistol from beneath his robes and shot himself through the head. The church wasn't used as a religious structure again until after it was rebuilt in 1813. By the end of the war, everyone that had known where the treasure was hidden was dead, and to this day the treasure hasn't been found. There are plenty of written records that my Daddy has photocopied and collected over the years to support everything I've just said."

Heather looked at Sarah and raised an eyebrow as though silently asking what she had gotten herself into. Sarah ignored her sister and smiled excitedly at Erin. "Wow, this place must be crawling with ghosts!"

Erin looked at her with a sad smile touched with an almost invisible hint of brooding terror. "Oh, it is crawling with ghosts. Take my word for it. If more people knew what goes on around there, the congregation would be afraid to show up on Sunday and my poor parents would be besieged by every ghost- hunter wannabe within a thousand miles. You can't do anything to get my father to go into that place after dark, and he's not afraid of anything. Daddy was a Navy Corpsman that got a whole pile of medals for valor while serving with the Marines in Vietnam. That's why a discreet group from out-of-state is perfect for handling this. My father just wants to have someone outside of his own family tell him he's not crazy and give him proof in writing."

Diana drove most of the way to Cleveland, then I took over just before the Interstate began paralleling the southern shore of Lake Erie. I handed the keys to Kim near Buffalo in New York, and then I fell asleep as she drove in the dark.

I slept fitfully, often awakening as the van moved down the long road. These dreams lacked the vivid, lifelike quality of the dream the night before, and were more in keeping with what one would normally expect from a dream in every way aside from their content and memorability.

I dreamed that I saw a robed king sipping wine from a heavy silver flagon, and he was surrounded by dancing satyrs that played shrill pan-pipes and beat wildly on drums around him. Wildly gyrating to the music, I saw legions of women dancing nude in the torchlight. Driven by a strange, ecstatic, trance-like madness, they gyrated with a manic enthusiasm that had a vaguely disturbing quality to it which I would be hard pressed to quantify or put to words. The wild drumbeats and the frantic piping were all identical to the music from my dream the night before. This was the tune to which I had mated with my own flesh and blood. Had the dream continued, without a doubt other women would have followed suit. I scanned the female faces before me, each one wild with animal passion.

The king looked at me and smiled pleasantly. He looked sincerely happy, but something about his gaze sent a chill down my spine. Among the dancers, I recognized my dear friend Diana, her body looking like a tattooed angel, and I took a moment to admire her nude body. Yes, she certainly did have some very nice tattoos in some very interesting places. I was shocked to see Erin's saintly, virginal body exposed to the world as she gyrated merrily among the other women. To my left, I saw my mother, my sister, my cousins, and my aunt dancing, swaying nude in the firelight.

The king, a well-muscled, bearded man with long white hair and flowing reddish-purple robes of shimmering, iridescent silk, approached me. "Forgive me for not introducing myself to you in your dream last night. You seemed... shall I say, occupied? I am Acratophorus, the giver of unmixed wine. Please forgive me for skipping the usual pleasantries and getting right to the point. In just a few minutes, the van you're in is going to hit a pothole in the road and you'll wake up, so we don't have much time." He spoke English with an accent that almost would have passed for a well-educated 21st century American, but layered beneath that accent I thought I detected almost imperceptible hints of British pronunciations and some strange vestiges of another accent that I could not place. He had used the word "van" with the same sort of emphasis that the elderly sometimes use when showcasing their knowledge of contemporary slang terms to younger people. It was as though he felt more pride in his ability to correctly identify the type of modern vehicle I was riding in than he did in his casual prediction that I would soon awaken because it would hit a pothole.

"I need some minor assistance with a small problem that I have, and in return I promise that I will bless you as I have not blessed anyone in centuries. You see, a few years ago, as a very good friend of mine, John Wilmot, the Second Earl of Rochester lay on his deathbed, a priest named Gilbert Burnet took something from him that belonged to me. When Bishop Burnet realized that he lacked the means to physically destroy it, he had it hidden in hopes that it would never be found again. Later, when I was hopeful that another worthy heir would find it, the priests moved the hiding place to yet another remote location. For four hundred years my hopes have been frustrated. And what have I ever wished for anyone other than happiness and freedom?" He gestured expansively and smiled at me. "You have one more test before I give my treasure to you along with all the honor and responsibilities that come with being my high priest. I'm an excellent judge of people, and I dare say that I know more about you than you know about yourself. After last night, I have no doubt that you'll enjoy the nature of this test and you'll meet my expectations with no difficulty at all, but you can't blame me for being too careful. I've been betrayed before, and I want to see how you will act when we raise the stakes a bit. Oh, yes, last night was only a very special and very realistic dream. Your little adventures last night didn't actually make anyone pregnant, although your sister found the experience realistic enough that she checked her hymen to make certain that it was still intact this morning, and she still felt a few aches as she went through today, although that was entirely in her own mind. And if you want to start a family with your cousin Heather, then you will have to take care of that later. I just let you and a few other people share a very special dream in a separate reality that I personally created just for the occasion. For now, I will need you to recover what was stolen from me. Oh, you'll know it when you see it, don't worry about that. I would describe it, but I am very certain that I would hate to ruin the surprise. I have great need for someone that I can trust to have this and put it to its proper use, and after last night I feel confident that you will serve my needs perfectly. I'm certain that this is an arrangement that will benefit us both." He winked at me with conspiratorial mirth, then glanced up at the sky with the air of a man checking his watch. "It was a pleasure speaking to you, but I must let you go. Your vehicle is moving with frightful rapidity, and you are only a few stadia away from the pothole that will awaken you. I shall see you again very soon. I promise." He smiled at me with the kindly pride of an elderly man regarding a grandchild's modest accomplishments in school. "For now, brace yourself. The moment I leave, these ladies will be upon you like the wild Maenads that you have read about in your books on Greek mythology. If you've forgotten what you read there, then please consider this a brief refresher course, minus some of the less pleasant details that I hope you will never need to worry about." I briefly wondered how far a "stadia" was, and while I remembered the word "Maenads" from Greek Mythology, I couldn't quite place it. I was about to ask him for some clarification when he turned his back and begin striding away from me and my thoughts left the subject immediately. The women that had been patiently standing nearby fell upon me like a pack of wolves. Their pretty faces were wild, twisted with insane lust. Their claw-like fingers, some carefully manicured with delicately painted nails, were clawing and tearing at my clothes. Their faces were set with savage intent, and I began looking forward to being raped by these women.

We had plans to camp for the night at the Montezuma National Wildlife Refuge in the Finger Lakes region of New York State. Apparently Erin's parents enjoyed birdwatching and had found a nice, out-of-the-way place to camp where we could park the van and get some sleep for the night without anyone bothering us. A large bump awakened me as the van ran over some hidden unevenness in the road. I didn't know how long I had been asleep, but it was pitch dark outside. Outside I saw dark trees framing a purple, starlit sky. Erin directed Kim to turn down a rough road that dead- ended in a grassy clearing surrounded by thick reeds and water. The moonlight was bright enough that we could see without our flashlights.

We made a small campfire. Erin had brought graham crackers, chocolate and marshmallows, and I had packed an earthenware jug of "Apple Pie", a beverage so named because despite its wicked alcohol content it was sweet enough that it tasted like molten homemade apple pie, especially when served warm. You can hardly tell the alcohol is there, which makes this a bit of a dangerous drink for the uninitiated.

(I make my Apple Pie drink a little differently every time, but I'll share the basic recipe with you. I use a half-gallon of apple cider, about a quart of apple juice, between three and five cinnamon sticks, just enough pumpkin pie spice that you can hardly taste it, and a splash of good vanilla extract that a friend of mine brought back from Mexico. Sweeten it to suit yourself, but I use roughly two cups of white sugar. My uncle, a crazy old bachelor that lives in a wooden shack by himself in the mountains of western North Carolina, prefers to use brown sugar, but I don't. Let it simmer in a slow cooker for a day or two on low, then fish out the cinnamon sticks or the cinnamon will get to overpowering the rest of the drink. Now, let it cool down so that the alcohol doesn't evaporate out after you add it, and if you want you can let it age for another one or two days in the refrigerator. Then decide how potent of a drink you want. I add about a quarter of a bottle of decent rum, about a quarter cup of cheap brandy, and then top it off with about a half-cup of any respectable vodka. My uncle prefers to just dump in half of a bottle of pure, 190-proof grain alcohol or spike it with a canning jar full of his homemade moonshine. Now, I love my uncle and I hate to sound cocky, but my uncle is crazy and you should make this drink my way because my way tastes better. Serve the drink warm, especially during the Fall and Winter. I use a slow- cooker on low, with the lid kept on so that the alcohol will re-condense instead of evaporating out, and we ladle it into coffee-cups. During the wintertime, I also make a homemade mulled wine that I ferment myself, but my family brought the recipe and the original yeast cultures over from Europe many years ago, and I'm not sharing the recipe with anyone.)

I built a small fire from oak twigs, then I loosened the cork in the jug of Apple Pie so that it wouldn't shoot out when the beverage began to heat up and set it down close to the fire. As I did this, Diana used her pocket knife to whittle some sticks into forks for the rest of the crew to use in roasting hot dogs and making s'mores. I knew Diana well enough to know that she would want to re-sharpen her knife after using it, and I also knew her well enough to know that she never packed a whetstone or a ceramic stick. Retrieving them from my rucksack, I wordlessly slipped them into the back pocket of her tight blue jeans. I didn't deliberately try to make any more contact than was necessary to slip her the sharpening supplies, but only a dead man could have failed to appreciate what the small amount of contact I had with her wonderfully firm ass cheek.

"Thanks!" Diana said as she smiled at me brilliantly. She didn't need to be told what I had just put in her back pocket. I had clearly read her mind.

Wedged in between the luggage and plastic storage bins full of the rest of our gear in the back of the van, we had a few folding chairs which the other ladies helped to set up in a ring around the campfire. Soon we were munching our dinner and sipping the hot, sweet apple-flavored beverage from the battered and fire- stained tin cups we used for camping. The faces around the campfire reflected the flickering light, and the memory of the torchlit scenes from my dreams came unbidden to my mind.

Kim walked over to the van, and pulled out a blue plastic storage bin. Diana and I both instantly began to rise to help her. "No, I've got it!" she grunted as she awkwardly lugged the plastic chest over to where Sarah and Heather were sitting. Both of my cousins glanced expectantly at the plastic chest.

Plopping herself down on the ground near the fire, Kim pried the lid off the storage bin and began pulling out items.

"Hey, Kim," Sarah asked. "Did you get a tattoo?"

My heart seemed to stop and a chill ran down my spine as I remembered the tattoo on my sister's left hip from my previous night's dream. I looked over, and as my sister had bent over to open the container her t-shirt had ridden up just enough to reveal the top of a tattoo on her left hip. Her pants covered most of it, but the part I saw looked dreadfully familiar.

Kim smiled at Sarah. "Yep!" And then she erased any further doubt in my mind by pulling the waistband of her jeans aside and showing Sarah her new tattoo, a small stylized heart with the words "Love is Forever" written around it in flowing script. My heart pounded inside of my chest. I didn't know what was going on, but there is no way that I could have known about that tattoo last night when I had seen it in my dream, looking exactly as it now did in real life.

"It just finished healing up," Kim said. "I've been waiting until it was healed up to tell people about it, since people always want to see a new tattoo and before it healed it just looked kind of gross." She reached into the container and pulled out a battered fanny pack made of nearly indestructible fake leather. A stencil on the top of the bag identified it as kit number 3 of the five spare kits of basic ghost-hunting gear that we keep on hand to loan out to people that don't have their own.

Kim began: "First things first: when you're ghost-hunting, you'll always be with a partner at all times. That way someone else can verify everything you see, and it's also important for safety reasons. Now, most people that do ghost-hunting a lot have their own kit, but you'll be using one of the club's extras. We keep everything together in a fanny pack for easy access." Kim unzipped the main pocket of the fanny pack. "In this pocket, there's a small notepad and two mechanical pencils for taking notes. Record anything unusual you encounter in the notepad as specifically as possible. For example, if you get a sudden temperature change, record the time, the starting temperature, the ending temperature, and the amount of time that elapsed. Whenever you see or hear anything unusual, write down specific times so that we can look for possible causes that aren't supernatural. Too much data is far better than not enough. Some people also use the notepads for automatic writing, but our club doesn't have anyone in it that really does that, and since both of you are just starting out with this I would really discourage trying it for now. For one thing, I don't like the idea of letting just any old spirit out there use my body for any reason, and for another thing it's too easy to get results that you either deliberately or unconsciously influenced."

She held up a narrow, foil-wrapped cylinder. "This is a chemlight. If the batteries in both your primary and alternate flashlights go dead, this will give you enough light to safely find your way out. You might find that batteries sometimes die a lot faster when you're ghost hunting than they usually do under normal circumstances. In this pocket, we've got spare double and triple A batteries. Almost all of our portable equipment runs off of one of those two types, and at least one of the two flashlights that everyone carries should take one of those two types of battery. That way we can all share batteries." She held up a small digital camera. "This is a cheap little digital camera. I'm sure you know how to use it. Whenever something unusual is going on, feel free to start snapping a few photos even if you don't see anything unusual. Sometimes you might luck out and get a picture of something that was in the room with you that you couldn't see. I know that some of the regular members of the team like to carry their fancy infrared cameras, and those usually do work a lot better for catching pictures of paranormal activity, but they're also a lot more expensive. There's a spare memory card in the same pocket as the camera. Don't be afraid to take lots of pictures, and don't hesitate to use the video feature if you think you might catch something interesting. This is a digital voice recorder," she said while holding up the same sort of recorder that some students at school use to record the lectures. "Some people use it as an alternative to the notepad when it's too dark to write things down, but the main thing we have them in the kit for is for use while looking for EVPs, or, oh, what does that stand for?"

Heather looked at Kim and raised an eyebrow. "I don't know how I feel about all of this 'something in the room with me that I didn't see' stuff."

I answered Kim. "EVP stands for Electronic Voice Phenomenon. You ask questions or talk into an empty room, and sometimes something will answer you. You won't hear anything while you're asking the questions, but when you play back the voice recording you'll hear it. Most of the time it's so garbled that it's hard to tell what it's saying, but on rare occasions you can hear it loud and clear. It's pretty cool when they answer the question, but don't be surprised when say something entirely irrelevant or incoherent. Don't ever try to contact any spirit that you suspect might be evil or demonic using EVP or anything else. If you're getting EVP recordings and start getting a feeling you really don't like, it's usually a good idea to stay calm and in control, stop what you're doing, tell your partner, and leave. There's no point in taking any chance of getting a negative spirit attached to you if you can help it. Oh, and don't ever try to get EVP recordings anywhere but where you're investigating. We don't pretend to understand much about how exactly this works, and most of the people that do think they understand it are too cocky for their own good. But if you look for EVPs in a place that isn't already reputed to be haunted, there's a good chance that spirits that want to communicate with you will move in looking for you, and they'll likely be hard to get rid of. And you don't want that. Some people might disagree with me, but I say to never look for EVPs in your own home under any circumstances."

Kim smiled at me. "Thanks, Egon."

Diane chuckled. "I think the clearest EVP we've ever gotten was a man's voice saying 'it's dark in here'. We were in a private residence, asking if he was the spirit of a man that had killed himself in that room, but apparently he thought that it was more important to make sure that we had noticed that the lights in the room weren't on. If I were personally ever going to go through the trouble of returning from the grave and I finally got a chance to communicate with the living from the other side, I would hope that I would have something better to say than that!"

Several members of the party chuckled. Heather wasn't among them. I smiled at the reference to the EVP, and sipped my warm apple-flavored drink. There was a lot of alcohol in it, and I felt a warm flush in my face. The fire popped loudly. Neither Diana nor I like sudden, loud noises, and we both flinched. But Heather was already trembling slightly, and at the sudden sound she spilled a bit of her drink on her lap. Sarah giggled at her sister, and Heather responded to her with a withering glare.

Kim continued digging through the bag. "Use the walkie-talkie to communicate with the rest of us. We keep them all on channel 3, unless we are getting too much interference. We probably won't have cell phone reception where we'll be going. Turn the walkie-talkies off when anyone around you is looking for EVPs, for obvious reasons. Most people carry their own EMF detector, but you don't really need one. The plastic hiking compass in your bag is also affected by electromagnetic abnormalities, but it doesn't have batteries that can die and, far more importantly for our purposes, it's cheaper. Compasses are one of the oldest pieces of ghost hunting equipment that people still regularly use. If the needle quits pointing north or starts to spin, it generally indicates that something freaky is going on. Or it can mean that you're near metal or something that generates electricity, so don't just chalk up your compass acting up to anything abnormal. Record what your compass did and the time it happened in your notebook. By itself, most people don't consider EMF readings or a compass acting up to be clear evidence of the paranormal, but it can give you a strong indication of where to look for it. Now, this is a digital thermometer that can quantify and assist in documenting sudden temperature changes. Again, a sudden temperature change isn't evidence by itself, but it can help you find evidence by letting you know that something unusual might be going on. Some people say that it gets colder when spirits suck heat out of the air or they can take power from electrical equipment so that they can get the energy to manifest themselves. The little spool of masking tape is for marking locations without damaging surfaces, and the plastic bag with toilet paper and adhesive bandages is there for your comfort. The whistle is in case your radio quits working and you need help immediately, so only blow it in an emergency."

Sarah spoke up. "Are we going to use Ouija boards and stuff like that? I tried one of those at a party once, and it just spelled something that looked like someone had a cat walk across the keyboard of their computer."

Erin answered her from her seat across the fire. "Some people like those, but nobody in our club is much of a fan. I've heard of too many people that have played around with those boards and have had trouble with negative, harmful spirits afterwords. The Ouija boards don't guarantee contact with anything evil or demonic, and choosing not to use one doesn't guarantee that you won't encounter evil or demonic entities. It's a tool like any other, and it's neither inherently good nor evil. But I've known about enough people that have been hurt using it that I'm personally not interested in giving it a try."

Sarah looked at her. "But you are going to go after EVP recordings? What's the difference?"

"There really isn't much of one from the standpoint of, either way, you're trying to contact spirits and you never know with any certainty who or what, if anything, is going to answer you. But Ouija boards can be manipulated by people moving the planchette to what they either deliberately want it to point to, or to what they subconsciously expect it to point to, so the results aren't as objective or empirical as we would like them to be. We try as much as possible to keep the techniques that we use limited to ones that we can't either deliberately or unconsciously manipulate. That's part of why our own club doesn't rely much on psychics or mediums that claim to talk to the dead, although some other clubs find them very useful. You can't usually prove whether the experience is genuine, or whether they believe themselves to be channeling a spirit when in fact it's wishful thinking on their part. We'll listen to psychics or mediums that feel like sharing things with us and we're always respectful of them, but we take what they say with a grain of salt."

Reaching back into the storage bin, Kim dug out one of our stationary cameras. "Obviously we can't be everywhere at once. This is an infrared video camera that we leave running all night. We're going to have several of these set up in potentially active areas where we won't have people. We used to use motion activated ones, but apparently they aren't always sensitive enough to get triggered by ghosts. A camera can't pick up everything, but it's a lot better than just leaving spots that we can't monitor entirely blind. Also, they are good for detecting animals, people that aren't related to the investigation, or anything else in the area that might help us to account for things that would otherwise be hard to explain. On every investigation, our goal is to go in with the assumption that there is a logical explanation for anything that happens, and we only assign a supernatural cause for things that we cannot find any other possible explanation for. As far as the specifics of what you'll be doing tomorrow night, I'm sure that either John or Diane will give you all of that information after we break up in teams to begin the investigation. Any questions so far?"

Sarah and Heather regarded her soberly. "I don't think so," said Heather quietly. Then she got up and poured herself another cup of warm, alcohol-laden apple drink. Her face looked white, and her hands were trembling.

"Heather, are you sure you want to do this?" Erin asked.

"Yeah, it's not too late for you to sit out the investigation if you're not comfortable doing it," Diana offered. Prior to the last minute personnel shortage that we experienced, Diana and I had agreed that this would be an excursion that only experienced members of the club would be coming on. Partly, that was because we wanted to do the most professional job for Erin's parents that we could. Partly, our decision was because this was not going to be an easy haunting. If half of what Erin and her family said about the old church was true, this was going to be one hell of a wild ride.

There are two major types of hauntings, depending on how you classify such things. Residual hauntings are by far the most common. You could compare them to watching an old recording of something that has happened in the past. They're usually more-or-less predictable, and you may encounter sights, sounds, smells, feelings, or other phenomena that don't have any rational explanation. Even so, residual hauntings are typically absolutely harmless. Whatever is happening there, it doesn't involve any sort of spirit that knows you're there or is interested in interacting with you for good or ill. They're usually good hauntings to use for training beginners.

Intelligent hauntings are different from residual ones. With intelligent hauntings, the spirit knows you're there and may be interested in interacting or sometimes even communicating with you. These are the hauntings that most people think of when they're thinking about ghosts. They can interact with objects, open and close doors, and they can also interact with people. Sometimes these hauntings are playful and harmless, and at other times they can be horrifying or even downright physically dangerous. There are some types of intelligent hauntings, such as demonic activity, that beginners should definitely not ever be involved with investigating. We didn't know for certain what we were getting into here. There were definitely going to be multiple spirits involved, and categorizing a haunting like this one is well-neigh impossible. The persistent fear that the haunting had seemed to inspire for over two centuries now was not a good sign at all.

My sister was probably experienced enough to hold her own, especially if there was someone more experienced than herself paired with her. I began to feel guilty for allowing my cousins to come with us and not speaking up in the restaurant this morning. Heather might get herself into trouble by panicking. Sarah could get herself into trouble by failing to take things seriously enough.

Sarah started to say something that probably would have been sarcastic, but Heather cut her off. "I'm fine. Really, I am. It's just that this stuff sounds a lot more... I don't know. It's creepier talking about this here in the woods in the dark than it was back at the restaurant this morning. And I thought we were just all walking around together looking for ghosts, but this is like your focus isn't on whether or not this stuff is real, but you're actually bringing along stuff to measure it, and acting like you know what you're looking for. That EVP thing really creeps me out, and I don't like the idea of being able to take pictures of stuff that I can't see but it's in the room with me."

"It's OK, Heather." I offered. I walked over and hugged my cousin. She hugged me back fiercely, her warm face brushed my own and her soft, slightly chubby body was pressing against me through her soft pink sweater. She trembled in my arms, and I felt her breath against my neck. I had been feeling guilty about letting her come along. Now, as my erection began to grow in my pants, I began to feel guilty about that as well. "You don't have to do anything you don't want to," I said as soothingly as I could.

"I'll be fine. Promise me you won't let me chicken out" Heather said to me with a nervous, mirthless chuckle.

I didn't reply. I'm not making any promises that I can't keep, and if Heather is scared then I'm not going to try to get her to come along. I love my cousin, and I won't hold her accountable for halfhearted bravery when she's getting a bit drunk and discussing something that she only halfway understands. I also don't want to take someone along on an investigation that might freak out, no matter how much they mean to me. I've seen people that are new to ghost-hunting that go absolutely bananas the first time they see something they weren't expecting, and it's never fun to try to deal with them. One hysterical person can easily accidentally hurt themselves or someone else, or they can ruin an entire investigation. It almost inevitably happens right when you are finding precisely what you came to look for. That's one of the many reasons that I like ghost- hunting with the seasoned crew that I'm used to.

Diana got up and refilled a large tin camping mug, the outside of which had been stained black by the flames of many campfires before this one. I wondered how many cups she had consumed already. She sure did look beautiful in the firelight. As a matter of fact, I think all of my companions did. I could tell that, as usually was the case on matters like this, Diana and I were thinking similarly about Heather. "We'll see how you feel tomorrow. I'm sure Erin still has friends in Vermont that she can call if we need someone to replace you." She glanced at me. "Hey, John, are you ready to help me set up the tent?"

As I walked off to assist Diana with the tent, I heard Erin assure Heather that not only would her elder sister be visiting from out-of-town, but she still had two or three good friends in the area that she could trust to help out without them talking too much about what they found to the rest of the locals.

The van is large enough to comfortably sleep three people on the floor and bench seats, but for a party of this size we usually set up a small tent that can comfortably sleep several more. As usual when we camped, I planned to sleep by myself in a jungle hammock I kept in my rucksack. It's quick and easy to set up if you know how to use it, it has a waterproof roof, mosquito netting on the side, and it keeps you from having to share a tent with other people, since I'm rather easily awakened. Diana and I took the clear storage container that contained the tent out of the van and moved towards a flat piece of ground a bit off of the road and safely away from the fire.

"That was pretty sweet how you were with your cousin. You're a pretty good guy, John." Diana said.

"Thanks." I responded as I began laying out the tent stakes and organizing shock-corded fiberglass poles. "You're pretty amazing yourself."

"John, we've been friends for a pretty long time." Diana's speech was a bit slurred. I loved her dearly, but I really did wish that she would get help with her drinking problem. Considering some of the things she'd been through in her life, I don't suppose that I can blame her.

"Yep. You're probably the closest buddy I've got." I was telling the truth.

"John, I love you. You know that, right?"

Friends always say thing like that, especially when they're drunk. I clapped her cordially on her shoulder in a you're-one-of-the-guys sort of way. "I love you too, buddy." I was feeling a bit uncomfortable, but, again, I was telling the truth. I loved her, definitely as a friend. Perhaps as something more than that if I were being completely honest. She was undoubtedly an extremely attractive woman. And I would be lying if I said that I didn't fantasize about making love to her on a fairly regular basis.

Diana is my closest friend, and we had made the commitment several years ago not to mess up our friendship with romance. Neither one of us had a good track record for romantic relationships that didn't end in complete disaster. She had been married before her first deployment with the military, and her husband had left her for another woman before she had returned. She had been faithful to him while she was enduring some of the most hellish conditions imaginable, and comfort could have been available to her in the form of any one of hundreds of healthy young men that hadn't had sex in a year and a half. Despite her healthy sex drive, she had remained chaste and loyal to her husband, and only discovered his perfidy after her return to the States. He had taken just about all of the money she had earned while overseas and spent it on himself and his new girlfriend. It was an understatement to say that he had clearly never deserved her.

Four months ago, Diana's most recent boyfriend had been lying in bed beside her one night when she was having nightmares, which isn't uncommon for either Diana or myself. Anyhow, the fool tried to wake her up by grabbing her face and shaking her. She hadn't meant to hurt him, but she was in the midst of a dream in which she had been fighting for her life, and she awoke not knowing at first where she was, who he was, or that he wasn't an enemy trying to kill, capture, or rape her. There was still a hole in the drywall about five feet from the bed where the top of his head had struck it. Luckily he didn't press charges, but he had angrily grabbed his stuff and left after screaming "You need help!" at her. I didn't want to agree with him, but I had been trying to get her to come to counseling at the VA for several years. Their PTSD counseling had helped me more than I ever expected, and I wished that she would give it a try as well. If nothing else, she needed to get her drinking under control. Oh, I'm talking about her demons here but trust me, I've got plenty of issues of my own.

Diana finished arranging the fabric portion of the tent, so that now all we had to do was stake it down and slide the flexible fiberglass poles through some loops in the tent and it would be ready, unless we felt the need to bother with the rain fly, which I didn't think we needed tonight.

I walked over to the tent with a handful of stakes, and Diana met me beside the tent and wrapped me into a warm hug. We were friends, and as such we hugged each other regularly, but this time the energy felt entirely different. She pressed more of her body against mine than usual, and buried her face in my neck. I couldn't tell for certain whether or not I felt light kisses against the side of my neck, but my cock immediately began to strain against the front of my pants. My heart was in my throat. She was pressed so close to me that I knew she could feel my hardness through her blue jeans. I found myself wishing that someone would come over from the fire to help us with the tent, saving me from an awkward situation. And, paradoxically, I found myself wishing that Diana and I would be able to spend the entire night alone together fulfilling dreams that we had both nurtured for far too long.

I told myself that I would definitely have to go into the woods and masturbate later; my penis was painfully erect, and I was so horny that it was physically painful. Diana moved her face from my neck, and began slowly moving her lips towards mine. I wanted to kiss her desperately, but she was drunk and I couldn't allow anything to happen that would jeopardize our friendship.

With a herculean exercise of raw willpower, I released my hold on the beautiful woman that I wanted just as badly as she wanted me. If Diana and I were going to go here in our relationship, it would be well-thought-out, discussed rationally, and we would most definitely make the decision together while we were both sober. No drunken make-out session or quick fuck was worth messing up my closest friendship.

I released Diana, but her arms remained wrapped around me as though she were drowning and clinging to me for dear life. I didn't want to, but I had to end the embrace before I kissed her or worse. I'm not the sort of man to take advantage of any drunken woman. And I would rather die myself than hurt Diana. Gently, I applied pressure to her shoulders to guide her away from me.

Without warning, my world spun around me. Wind rushed in my ears, and in far less than a second I found myself flat on my back on the tent fabric. As a martial artist myself, I had instinctively reacted to Diana's artful throw, and I had executed a breakfall. Diana had thrown me and now had me pinned to the fabric of the tent, her sweet body pressing hard against mine. My martial arts experience is predominantly in taekwondo, which is great if you want to kill or injure someone. While, like most modern martial artists, I get a more well-rounded education than some people give us credit for (hence knowing how to take the throw without getting hurt), taekwondo is almost useless against an aikido expert unless you're willing to hurt or kill them. And I would never do anything to harm Diana. I felt her full weight pressing down upon me, her face less than an inch from mine, her warm breath caressing my face. She was heavier than she looked. I was acutely aware of the crotch of her tight blue jeans pressing against my rock-hard dick through my pants.

"Tell me you don't want this and I'll stop," she breathed. "But first, I am going to kiss you. And if I have ever meant anything to you, even as a friend, then please, I need you to kiss me back. Just once. It won't kill us. Then we can go back to the way things have always been. Please do this for me." I felt her warm, soft, slightly moist lips brush mine.

"Diana, I'm sure that would be awesome, but you're drunk and I'm not-" I started to reply before her soft lips touched mine again, this time planting an airy, chaste kiss that sent electricity through my whole body and caused my heart to skip a beat. Then, my capacity for rational thought was obliterated as her lips crushed hard against mine. I felt her crotch grind hard against my own, and a sudden, overpowering flood of testosterone in my bloodstream washed away my ability to think like a flash flood carrying away a pile of twigs. Madly, I reached behind her, my hand feeling her soft dark hair as I pulled her sweet, precious face to mine.

Diana's hot, wet tongue and mine mingled together, and I savored everything about how the kiss tasted and felt. Every drop of her saliva that she shared with me was a gift more precious than diamonds. With my left hand, I pulled her face closer to mine, wanting this kiss to be as deep as possible, to last as long as it possibly could. Our teeth clicked together painlessly. My other hand went lower, and cupped the delicious curve of an ample butt cheek. If this was the only kiss I was ever going to get from her, and it was too late to avoid it, then I may as well make sure that it would be worth remembering and count on the strength of our friendship to avoid letting things get awkward tomorrow. She now ground herself rhythmically against me, her soft, sensual, feminine curves driving me wild with desire. Any pretense that this was not sexual was long gone. If she kept this up I was pretty sure that we were both going to climax, even if the clothing between us remained in place. And our clothing remaining on for much longer seemed highly unlikely.

I flipped her onto her back and pinned her to the tent fabric without breaking the kiss, and she voiced her approval with an appreciative hum. I felt her soft hands press under my shirt and roam my back. Her legs wrapped around my waist. Our tongues ravaged each others' mouth as my hand lifted the hem of her t-shirt, caressing the smooth milky softness of her belly. Beneath her shirt, my hand went higher. My heart pounded in my chest as I felt the satin softness of a bra- clad breast. Her hand caressed my turgid bulge through the cloth of my cargo pants. My heart was in my throat as my hand slipped under the wire that supported the bottom of her bra, and I ran my calloused fingers across her exquisitely soft breast and rubbery nipple. She gasped sweetly, and I kissed her gently on the neck. It is anyone's guess where this would have led had we not been interrupted.

"Hey, horndogs!" I heard my cousin Sarah's voice. "If that's how you're trying to get the tent set up, then I think you read the directions wrong." I have always loved my cousin, and while I would never literally throw her into a wood-chipper, there are times when joking about it isn't out of the question. Although I was as sexually frustrated as I had ever been in my life, I knew that Sarah was probably saving Diana and I both from making a very significant mistake. I would never want to be something that Diana regretted the next morning. Diana and I looked over and saw Sarah and Heather standing there together.

"Uh... do you need some help putting the tent together?" Heather asked in an unusually husky-sounding voice. Was she turned on by watching us?

Diana smiled at me ruefully as we struggled to our feet, dusted ourselves off, and rearranged our clothing.

"We would love some help putting the tent together," I offered with a voice that came out in something like a croak. I was pretty worked up.

With four people working at it, the tent was set up rapidly. For good measure, since we had extra help, we even attached the rain fly.

"Where do you guys have the sleeping bags?" asked Sarah. She had been in the bathroom when we were talking about that. Hadn't anyone gotten the word to her?

"We were supposed to bring our own. I just brought some sheets, a pillow, and some blankets," Heather responded.

"Well, that's crap!" Sarah said with annoyance. "I thought that there were some extra sleeping bags that belonged to the club! I just brought my own pillow for sleeping in the van."

"There are extra sleeping bags," I offered, "but we needed to know that you needed to borrow one before we left, so that we would know to pack one for you." I still felt lightheaded from the encounter with Diana, and

I didn't think my voice sounded quite right yet. My erection still hadn't entirely subsided.

It wasn't too cold outside, but a sleeping bag would probably help Sarah to sleep more comfortably. Yes, I'm closer to my sister and Heather, but I still love Sarah dearly and she'll always be my cousin. The weather wasn't particularly bad for upstate New York. I had an insulated vest and a jacket, and I supposed that if worst comes to worst I could use the hammock as a blanket. "Here, just use my sleeping bag for tonight. I'm sure that when we get to Erin's parents' place they'll have all the sheets and blankets we need."

"You're awesome, cousin!" Sarah beamed at me cheerfully.

"What about John? What's he going to do tonight?" Heather asked her sister reproachfully.

"I'm tough, don't worry about me. And it's not too cold out, considering," I said. I glanced around. Where had Diana gone? I headed for the van to get my sleeping bag for Sarah, and I caught up with Diana. She was busy hauling her own gear out of the back of the van.

"Hey, Diana"

Diana smiled at me. Reaching out, she sweetly patted me on the side of the face. "Sorry about that. I know it's confusing. Thanks for everything: both telling me no because I'm drunk and for letting me kiss you. I needed both."

"Well, my main concern is that you're my best friend, and I can't risk anything screwing that up. And, if we do get physical, I want us to both be sober when we do it."

"You're my best friend, too." she whispered. "And I don't want anything to screw up our friendship, either. If we're just friends from here on out, then that's just fine and I'm glad that we both got to share the kiss. I don't regret it and I don't think I would have ever regretted what we were about to do if we hadn't been interrupted, either." She winked at me. "But you're right. At least for now, until I get myself sorted out, can we go back to the way things were?"

"So you want to be just friends for now, and maybe talk it over later?"

"Sounds great." she sounded relieved. "You're not mad at me for how I acted? First I damned near raped you, and now I'm leaving you with a killer boner and no relief! You know that I didn't plan any of that."

"If you couldn't tell, I didn't exactly mind." I said, feeling as though a great weight had been lifted. Apparently any threat to our friendship had passed.

"You'll always be my buddy, John."

"And I'll always be yours."

"So do you think your boner is going to kill you?"

I laughed. "I'll live. And you've given me some memories to help me take care of it myself in the woods later."

She laughed, but I suspected that she was thinking similarly. She hugged me, this time just a friendly hug. "Good night, John. We'll talk about this some time later, when we're both sober and well-rested."

"Good night, Diana."

That night I shared the tent with Sarah and Kim, both of whom looked snug and warm beneath their ample bedding. It usually gets a little chilly at night in upstate New York in the spring, but there was something unnatural in the air that night. As soon as we were all lying down to go to sleep, the temperature seemed to perceptibly plummet at a rate that defied any rational explanation. Within a few minutes of lying down, I could clearly see my breath. Within an hour, I felt very certain that the temperature was well below freezing. Soon the thick night air had become bitterly, unnaturally cold. Through the windows of the tent, I could see a dense, foggy miasma that had rolled in off of the lake, and it glowed eerily in the dim moonlight.

I was wishing that I had asked to sleep in the van, but I didn't wish to disturb Diane, Heather, and Erin. The temperature had suddenly dropped to such an extreme low that I was genuinely worried about frostbite, and the frigid air that flowed in from the lake made certain that the icy, biting fangs of razor-sharp cold easily penetrated my futile attempts to insulate myself. And how the hell was a breeze blowing inside of a tent, when there were no apparent winds outside? Despite my jacket and vest, and having covered myself with a thin Army poncho and the jungle hammock, I was huddled into a fetal position and shivering uncontrollably. Worse yet, the waterproof nylon fabric that made up the poncho and the roof of the hammock rustled with the slightest movement when it wasn't being suspended from a tree, and I was afraid of disturbing my companions.

I didn't know what time it was when I heard Kim moving in her sleeping bag. I was about to head to the van to see if I could find a warmer place to sleep, when Kim spoke. "Screw this, guys. I have never seen the temperature drop so much so quickly before in my life, and I'm headed to the van to get warm. John, you're tougher than turtle tits for taking this damned cold without a sleeping bag! I'm freezing my ass off, even with one! I don't know why the hell you gave yours to Sarah. She's the one who didn't pack a sleeping bag." Kim was normally much kinder than that, but people sometimes say things they normally wouldn't when they're exhausted and uncomfortable. With that, she dragged her sleeping bag over to the door and I felt a severely bitter rush of even more brutally frigid air as she unzipped the door to the tent. Her numb fingers had difficulty grasping the zipper, and it took her several tries to get it open. She never did succeed in getting it entirely shut before she shuffled off on stiff, frozen legs for the van.

"Yeah, well, that's because your brother is nicer than you are!" Sarah yelled drowsily after Kim. She didn't sound cold at all, which surprised me. The sleeping bag that I had packed for myself was only of medium weight, and it still should have felt a bit chilly in there.

The fact that my sister had just paid me a compliment regarding my toughness delayed my joining her by mere seconds. Before I could get up and follow Kim, a flashlight clicked on from where Sarah lay on the floor and shone in my face. I covered my eyes against the glare of the sudden light, and was aware of frozen condensation glittering from the surface of my poncho. Looking around, the inside of the tent was covered with a thick dusting of sparkling crystalline frost that gave it some resemblance to the inside of an icebox. I have camped with tents many times over the years, and no matter how thick the frost gets outside of the tent I have never seen it form like this inside of one, even when the temperature is well below zero. Condensation might freeze inside of a tent, but frost just plain can't form like this. I had checked the weather before we left, and I felt certain that I had read that tonight was only supposed to have a low of 45 degrees Fahrenheit. It wasn't even supposed to get down to freezing tonight, and just a few hours ago it had been downright pleasant outside. Something bizarre was going on here.

"So, John, you really must be freezing your ass off. I feel like crap for taking your sleeping bag." Sarah said.

"I'm a bit cold." I stammered laconically, trying to keep my voice even. I'm sure it trembled despite my best efforts. I was most definitely well into a state of mild hypothermia. Even with the sleeping bag, I wondered how Sarah wasn't freezing her butt off. Looking around, I saw that the frost had formed everywhere in the tent with the exception of the immediate area where Sarah was sleeping. Could it have possibly been physically colder where Kim and I were lying than it was where Sarah was? That was impossible! What was going on here?

"Come over here. There's room in your sleeping bag for both of us if we scrunch in close," Sarah offered.

I was in no position to refuse her. Gratefully abandoning the hammock and poncho that I had been attempting to use as a blanket, I climbed across the slippery frost-covered tent floor, took my shoes off, and began climbing into my sleeping bag with Sarah.

"Holy shit, your jacket is freezing!" Sarah exclaimed. Sarah, as usual, was sleeping in a well-worn oversized T-shirt and her socks and underwear. Apparently that was insufficient protection against precisely how cold my jacket had gotten.

"Sorry, Sarah." I peeled off the jacket and my vest, and placed them on the floor beside the sleeping bag. I immediately felt the warmth of her body heat, and it was a definite improvement.

"John, the outside of your pants is pretty cold, too. Especially the buttons and your belt buckle. Can't you just sleep in your underwear?"

"You've done the laundry over at our house enough times to know that I don't wear it." I replied. There was a long moment of silence as we huddled together inside of the sleeping bag. My body felt as though it was thawing out from being frozen, and it felt amazingly good to be warming up again. My fingers tingled painfully as feeling returned to them.

"So, John," Sarah whispered in a vaguely accusatory tone, "I thought that you and Diana weren't dating." "We're not. We're just really good friends. What you saw was... well, she was drunk, and she said that she just wanted to kiss just once. I suppose just to see what it was like. She didn't really give me much of a choice in the matter, but we're still just good friends."

"You looked like awfully good friends from what I saw."

I was confused enough on my own about what had happened with Diana. My cousin's interest was understandable, but she wasn't helping me to feel any better. "We are very good friends, but it's not like what you seem to think. I love her dearly, but we agreed a long time ago that we're not going to date each other. We'll discuss it later, but she's never acted like that before and it's likely she never will again now that she's gotten that out of her system. To tell you the truth, Sarah, if I'm only going to get one chance in my life to make out with my best friend, I wish that you and Heather had been kind enough to at least give me a few more minutes. I suppose that it's pretty obvious that she and I have romantic feeling for each other, but our friendship is more important to us, and if we are going to risk what we've already got between us to start dating then there's no need to rush the thought process."

"Oh, I'm sure that you'll have other opportunities to kiss her. I've tried that just-kiss-once thing before, and it never works. I think that the very fact that you are both trying something new and exciting while saying that you'll never get to do it again at the same time is a pretty sure formula for keeping you thinking about it and wanting more of it for a long while afterwords."

I chuckled. "Not always, Sarah. Remember when we were kids and wanted to be able to tell people that we had kissed someone, so we made a deal to kiss each other on the lips for five seconds straight, and then never tell anyone who our first kiss had been with? That was totally innocent." Maybe I was being a bit clueless, and maybe I was being less than entirely honest. I had been young, but not so young that locking lips with my attractive cousin hadn't excited me. I have always been closer friends with her older sister, Heather, but Sarah was always by far the wilder of the two, and was more likely to go along with things that could potentially get us into trouble. Heather was definitely the good one, but Sarah was always up for crazy adventures.

"Of course I remember that. And, at the risk of freaking you out, especially considering our sleeping arrangement for the night, that really did... impact me. And don't pretend that it didn't change the way you looked at me for a long time afterwords! I still sometimes catch you checking out my ass, which I don't think you ever did before that kiss, so don't pretend otherwise!"

I started to reply, but Sarah continued. "Now, don't start apologizing or trying to deny it! It makes me feel good that you look at me in that way. And, you know what? The first time I really did kiss a guy, I was wishing that it could be you."

I smiled. "That's pretty cool. Thanks for telling me that. You know, in all honesty, I enjoyed our kiss together more than I've ever let on. I suppose that there have been a couple of times over the years when I've been kissing a girl and I've thought of that first kiss with you back when we were kids."

In the dark, she turned and looked at me for a long moment. She reached over and put an arm across me. "Do you think we could try that kiss again?"

I chuckled. "Sure. Five seconds again?" I naively thought that she was interested in playfully re-living a cute, innocent event from our childhood. Rolling over, I gave her a light peck on the cheek.

"Yep. Five seconds," she murmured as our lips brushed in the dark.

For a moment, we just held our lips together, moving them ever so slightly in slow kisses that somehow seemed all the more erotic because of their deliberate innocence. She inhaled deeply as her lithe arms encircled my back, crushing me to her. Her lips moved slowly against mine, and I immediately felt myself melt into a kiss that was anything but a childish stunt. Her hands traveled under my shirt, her warm skin feeling soft against my back. Her wet lips parted, and I tasted her mouth for the first time. Her saliva was like an intoxicating beverage as our moist tongues caressed each other. We were well over five seconds already, and this kiss was in every way different from the last one so many years earlier. We broke the kiss as she pulled my shirt over my head and climbed on top of me, her soft cotton panties pressing hard against the crotch of my pants, and I could feel my cousin's rock-hard nipples crushing against my chest through her t-shirt. Through the two thin layers of fabric that separated our genitalia, I felt her warmth and knew that I was pressing into the softness of her nether region. Even that miniscule amount of penetration, so slight as to be nothing but symbolic in scale, seemed to flood my heart with thoughts that we had already crossed some nameless boundary.

I don't know which of us initiated the next kiss, but it was even more passionate than the one before it. Wet, delicious, and wicked, the incestuous kiss between cousins quickly had my head swimming in delightful hormones. With one hand I pulled her face to mine, deepening the forbidden kiss, and with the other hand I reached down, cupping the firm, pert roundness of her butt against me. Her over-sized t-shirt had ridden up, and through the soft cotton panties I could feel her ass with enough detail to fuel my lust to a fever-pitch. And the areas that her panties didn't cover ensured that, in some areas at least, I was feeling actual butt- cheek. Going for broke, I slid my hand inside of her panties, savoring the feel of her soft round ass. We continued to kiss, and I needed more.

This might be the only time I would ever get to be with Sarah. Pulling her face hard against mine, I reached with some difficulty between our writhing bodies, and was soon feeling her pussy through her panties. She gasped into my mouth as I pushed the crotch of her panties aside. I felt the soft, trimmed pubic hair of her vulva, and then my heart and mind felt as they might explode as I touched my cousin's moist vaginal entrance for the first time. Sarah broke this kiss, and gently pushed my head down upon the pillow we were sharing. In the dimness of the tent I saw my cousin's head silhouetted black against the barely glowing fabric of the tent roof above her. Again, for a very long moment, we simply looked at each other, and I halfway expected a gentle rebuke for my lack of self-control. Instead, she lowered her face to mine. This kiss was softer, gentler, and sweeter than its predecessors. As we kissed, I slowly worked a finger into her moistening tightness, savoring every detail of how she felt. Soon, the few drops of water-like liquid inside of her were replaced with a large quantity of a thicker lubrication. Sarah's body had figured out what was coming even before I knew for sure myself, and was preparing her for the incestuous act that was now all but inevitable. I felt almost crushed when she raised her hips, reached down, and gently removed my hand from her vagina. Returning her crotch to mine she began slowly, rhythmically rocking herself against me.

Placing her sweet lips close by my ear, so close that I felt the air of her breathy whisper wash over the skin of my face, she spoke. "Yes, I was fantasizing about you when I got my first kiss. I did the same thing when I was older and I lost my virginity." She emphasized her words with an overt grinding motion between her crotch and mine. As though she wished to eliminate any possibility that I might fail to understand this earth-shattering confession, she continued. "John, I was wishing it could have been you that took my virginity. I still wish that you and I had lost our virginity together, rather than throwing it away with people that aren't even in our lives anymore."

"You were thinking of me while you lost your virginity?" I whispered, somewhere between dumbfounded and awestruck.

The rubbing between our crotches briefly stopped. "Yes, I was." Sarah said matter-of-factly. "As much as you and Diana already mean to each other, you've probably given her a crush on you for the rest of her life with that whole once-in-a-lifetime kiss stunt. And, if you want to, I'm sure that you'll be fucking her soon enough that my little intrusion probably didn't really change anything aside from ensuring that the tent was set up before it got too much later."

My erection was pressing unbearably into Sarah's softness through my pants. She realized this, and moved herself against me again, forcing my erection to nudge deeper against her sex. In a sense, my penis was already, albeit to a limited extent, standing just inside the doorway to Sarah's vagina. In a sense, she and I could say that we were already making love. Yes, thin cloth was separating us just as a condom might, but my penis was still inside of her. I trembled with unbearable need.

"So, here you are making out with your cousin. Diana got you all worked up and then left you high and dry, and you're worried that if you go into the van, wake her up, take her into the woods and fuck her senseless like both of you really need, then it will somehow ruin your friendship with her. I understand, and the way we're all dressed it's too cold for that anyway. For now, though, this cock of yours feels like it needs release. What if you and I just kept progressing along the road we're already traveling? You're family, and nothing can ever change that. You'll always be family; it's not like I can somehow de-cousin you, or remove the DNA we share from the nucleus of every cell in our bodies. We've always loved each other, and we always will no matter what happens, so this is perfectly safe. You would be able to get off, and you would be giving me something that I've wanted for years. There's no risk to any friendship. Nothing would change, aside from since I took care of you when you were super-horny and needed nothing more than a nice fuck, you would owe me a good, solid fucking the next time I needed one. Family always takes care of each other, right? You've already spent most of the last five minutes finger-banging me and dry-humping with me. I don't imagine that finishing up the old-fashioned way would hurt anything. Sound like a deal?"

Her panty-clad pussy rubbed against the length of my cock. My mind was swimming, and I instinctively knew that I was in a position where I might very easily do something foolish that I would regret later. I struggled for sanity, but my body was demanding that I make love to my cousin. The age old need to mate, as essential to our species' survival as the need to eat and drink, was drowning out my desperate efforts to think logically. I couldn't think of a reasonable rebuttal to anything Sarah had said. I wanted this at least as badly as she did. But I knew that I wasn't thinking logically. No man can think logically when all of his blood is pulsing inside of his rampant erection, which in turn is so close to the heavenly pussy of a beautiful woman. I knew this, and it scared me.

"Uh, Sarah? I don't have a condom, and I don't think..."

"Shhhhh. Don't worry, I'm on the pill, and you know me too well to be afraid of any dread diseases. This needs to be special. No other protection than the pill, and when you're ready, I want to feel you cum inside of me. I've never let anyone do that before you. Have you ever had unprotected sex before?"

I was honest. "Remember that girl that I lived with last year? She was on the pill, and we quit using condoms for a while until I realized that she wasn't as consistent with taking the pill as she said that she was, and I started insisting on a condom after that so that she didn't get pregnant. Apparently, her family had a long tradition of marriages that stemmed from unplanned pregnancies, and I didn't want to take any chances of her following in their footsteps."

"Well, I can assure you that I am very consistent with my birth control pills. No incest bastards for us, or anyone forcing you to marry your cousin. But you're going to be the first guy whose cock is actually going to get to feel my insides with nothing in between us. You'll be the first guy ever to cum inside of me. Does that turn you on?"

"Sarah, right now, everything about you turns me on. So we're cousins with benefits from now on?" My finger was still wet from her vaginal fluids, and I couldn't resist tasting her. I raised my hand to my mouth, which was difficult in the tight quarters we were in, and I breathed in her pheromone-laden musk as I tasted her. Any doubt that I had previously had about whether or not Sarah and I were going all the way tonight was erased as I smelled her pussy and licked her delightful honey from my finger. I needed her. Now.

Sarah laughed melodiously, then kissed me again on my lips. "Yep. From now on, we're kissin' cousins and fuckbuddies. Your cock is mine anytime I want it, and my pussy is yours whenever you want it. We love each other, and this is how things ought to be. We should have been doing this for years before now." I noted with approval the change to the one-for-one terms we had previously agreed upon.

"What if one of us gets married some day?"

"I can behave myself if you get married and don't want to play. But I can also share as long as you can, and nobody can stop us from visiting each other. After all, we're family." She seemed to relish every syllable of her wicked answer.

Sarah climbed off of me and began unbuckling my sturdy, nylon belt. Helping her, I began shucking my pants down into the bottom of the sleeping bag as she pulled off her shirt. Briefly, the sleeping bag was exposed to a rush of the bitter, unnaturally cold outside air. Then, the sleeping bag closed again with her on top of me and I felt myself surrounded by her soft skin and body heat. The only things that either of us were wearing were her socks and her cotton panties. In the dark, I saw my cousin's familiar face descend towards mine and felt wet, sultry lips pressing hard against my mouth. We kissed, deeply, passionately, wickedly, incestuously, as each of us let our hands explore the entire body of our new lover.

Sarah was a slender, petite woman. My hand followed the curve of her back, down to the twin hills of her glorious ass. My beautiful young cousin's tongue Writhed in my mouth, wrestling with my own. Her hot nipples pressed into my chest, and her soft brown hair tickled my face. Through her soft panties I felt the folds of her vaginal slit envelop my naked cock, which her body had pressed tight against my abdomen, and I thrilled to the feeling of the humid waves of warmth that washed over me from her sex. My head swam as her sweet fluids began to soak through her panties. My penis, for the first time, became moist with the sweet issue of my cousin's delightful pussy, which now mingled with my own pre-cum where our fluids met on the outside of her panties.

My hands reached down, again slipping into her underwear. She responded by reaching down and wriggling out of her panties, then planting a wet, sloppy kiss on my mouth as her hard nipples pressed against my chest and I felt, for the first time, the actual softness of skin-to-skin contact with my cousin's genitalia. Our kisses drove us mad with desire as she rubbed herself along the length of my cock, which was still straining as she pressed it against my abdomen. Her vagina was sopping wet, painting the bottom of my shaft with a magical mixture of her vaginal fluids and my own precum. Drifting up from the sleeping bag was Sarah's familiar scent, maybe consisting of her shampoo, body wash, and deodorant, mixed with the unmistakable erotic musk of an aroused woman. Dreaming about incest was one thing. But here in this sleeping bag, my sexual fluids were already mixing with hers. In the darkness, I felt more than saw Sarah look into my eyes. "I love you, cousin," she whispered. And then she raised her hips, reached down, and guided my rock- hard manhood into her heavenly depths.

Sarah was unbelievably wet. I drove myself up into her as she pounded her pussy down upon me. Wet, slapping sounds filled the tent and I hoped that they wouldn't be audible to those nearby in the van. My hands roamed her nubile body, delighting in her ass, her firm tits, and finally her face, which I pulled in to my own in a deep, sensual kiss. Our ability to move and choose positions was limited by the fact that we were in a sleeping bag and neither of us wanted the outside air getting in. Her body and mine were coated in a fine, slick layer of perspiration that added lubrication to every square inch of contact between us. Her lips pressed hard against the side of my face, and her sodden pussy made delightfully wet squishing sounds as she ground herself hard against my pubic bone. She was now making cute, breathy, soft grunting noises as our bodies merged, her breathing becoming harder. We were soon fucking with increasingly frenzied passion, her delicious young body leaking her inner moisture onto me as she rubbed, rocked, and pounded her sopping vulva against me.

I thought briefly about the friends and relatives that we had in the van nearby. They were probably sleeping soundly, unaware that just a few feet away from them two cousins, blood-relatives that had known each other their whole lives, were changing their comfortable familial relationship forever with an act of passionate, unprotected, incestuous sex that was coupled with promises that this act would be repeated many, many times.

Clenching her arms tightly around me, Sarah began shaking like an epileptic and her grunts became louder. Even in the dark I could tell that her cute face was being scrunched up in some unimaginable way. Her ass cheeks tightened and her slender legs clenched powerfully around my hips. I felt her sopping wet vagina clench and spasm around my manhood as her body trembled from what was quickly growing into an ecstatic, mind-blowing orgasm. My cousin, a dear friend and companion since childhood, was cumming on my hardness, blessing me with the precious gift of the most intimate of shared moments, giving me a part of herself in the form of a bountiful quantity of her precious girl-cum. It was the most erotic thing that I had ever personally experienced, and I couldn't hold back any longer. Hours of pent-up sexual tension flooded in powerful spurts deep into her beautiful young body as our mating reached a glorious mountaintop of ecstasy. I wanted to warn her, in case she had changed her mind and wanted me to pull out, but all that I managed was the strangled gasping of her name as I exploded with potent jets of my hot semen deep into the core of her thirsty, waiting depths.

"That's right, cousin! Cum inside me, fill me up, pour it into me! Oh, that's it! Oh, God, yes! That pussy is yours now, cousin! I love you!" she whispered breathlessly. I needed no encouragement. I sucked delicious lung- fulls of the icy air as spurt after spurt of my sperm-rich semen washed her sweltering insides. My cock continued to be bathed by her magical secretions and caressed by her glorious vaginal walls as they fluttered against me.

Several minutes passed before rational thought returned to either of us. Our bodies were spent like two deflated balloons, and she lay on top of me, my slowly softening member still embedded in her and our bodies sticking pleasantly together, adhered by our sweat. She lay on top of me, her firm breasts pressed hard against my chest, and I could feel her heart still pounding from the excitement and exertion of our lovemaking. I breathed in deeply, savoring the heady natural aroma of our bodies' incestuous union. Our breathing and heart-rate were slowly returning to normal.

"I love you, too, Sarah." I kissed her again. The aftereffects of my orgasm had me barely able to think or talk. Her vaginal walls still occasionally twitched and contracted around my manhood, and her insides were so moist with our shared fluids that it felt as though my gradually softening member might be pushed from my cousin's body simply by her sheer tightness.

She kissed me again on the lips, gently and sweetly. "Thank you, John."

"No. Thank you, Sarah. That was amazing." I whispered. Whoever said that thanking someone for sex is wrong had clearly never received it as the precious gift that it sometimes can be. My cousin had just given me something unspeakably rare and beautiful by sharing herself with me the way she had, and I would be a fool not to be grateful.

As always, rational thought returns slowly after an orgasm. I didn't regret what Sarah and I had just done, and knowing her as I did I doubted that it would cause trouble between us in our relationship. If anything, sex was something that would bond us closer together in the future. The knowledge that I would fall asleep with her fluids slowly drying on me, and the knowledge that she would fall asleep cuddled against me with a womb full of my sperm, made me feel closer to her in some sort of intangible manner. The union of our fluids seemed almost to have performed some magical alchemy that had forever linked us together in an arcane way that both strengthened and transcended our existing familial bonds.

"No, John, thank you. As crazy as it sounds, having sex with you is all I've been able to think about all day. I had a really weird and extremely vivid dream last night. You were in the woods in a clearing and you were having sex with all these different girls, and I was lying underneath you the whole time, I don't know, like humping myself against your back. Something was stopping me from moving out from under you or even talking to you. All I could do was hold you in my arms and try to get myself off by humping your back, but I never managed to get there. You know how dreams are sometimes. It damned near drove me crazy! Don't get mad, but one of the girls I dreamed you had sex with was Heather, and both of our mothers were telling you to do it. Trust me, you really don't want to hear who the other two you fucked before I woke up were, and I think my mom was going to fuck you next! You've always been closer to Heather than you have been to me, and I've never really minded it, but when you were fucking her while I had to lie beneath you like a damned mattress, and I couldn't get any relief while she got to feel your cock cum inside of her, I couldn't stand it. She's always had a crush on you, but she's scared to say anything, and she will never have the guts to actually do anything about it. Well, now she gets to fuck you in my dreams, but I am going to fuck you in real life! I'm prettier than she is, anyway."

"Hey. You know that I've always loved you, and you are drop-dead gorgeous. But Heather's pretty, too. Please just try to be nice when you talk about her; you know how close she and I have always been."

Sarah didn't reply, and I didn't want to press the issue. I really saw no point in upsetting Sarah or starting an argument. Sarah and Heather had always been rivals, with most of the rivalry existing on Sarah's part as though she were always determined to show-up her older sister. I didn't like it, but I had long ago accepted the dynamic as unchangeable. I loved them both, and just wished that they would get along.

After recognizing Kim's tattoo from my dream, I was less shocked than you might imagine by Sarah having shared the same dream that I had experienced, and now I knew who the girl beneath me that I never got to see was. It was still unusual to hear Sarah talking about the dream, though, while my penis was actually still inside of my own cousin. But with each passing second that our bodies lay together as one, it seemed more and more natural. Yes, Sarah and I were definitely going to have sex again many times. I wondered if my mother, Heather, and Kim remembered the same dream, and if so, how they felt about it.

Sarah rolled off of me, and I groaned almost painfully as my cock was deprived of her warm, moist tunnel. She cuddled naked against me, her vagina slowly leaking our mingled juices onto my leg. It felt good to feel the warmth and softness of her skin with absolutely nothing separating us, and I savored the way it felt to hold her gently and protectively against myself while relaxing in the afterglow of our lovemaking. I felt physically satiated as I hadn't been in years, and emotionally elated by the notion that so many physical and emotional boundaries with my cousin had just been erased.

"Sorry for talking like that about Heather, cuz. I know- Hey, did you just hear something outside of the tent?" Sarah whispered suddenly.

I listened carefully, but couldn't hear anything that sounded out of the ordinary. I will readily admit that I don't have the best hearing in the world. "I didn't hear anything. What did you think you heard?"

"It sounded like heavy breathing and a rustling sound." Sarah replied, seriously. After a moment, she broke into a wide grin and a wicked chuckle as she wrapped her arms around me. "It was probably just my imagination. Here I am, fucking my cousin within a few feet of both my sister and yours, not to mention a bunch of your friends. We could have been caught at any time! What would they think if they knew that we were fucking? Oh, my God! Can you even think of anything hotter than what we just did?" Sarah licked my earlobe.

I grinned at her conspiratorially. "That was awesome, cuz. But as cold as it was inside of the tent, I hate to think of what it would be like outside of it. I've honestly never seen weather act like this before in my life! I'm sure that they're all inside of the van, cuddled as deep within their sleeping bags as they can get."

Sarah reached into the sleeping bag, hunting for something. "I'm going to use my panties to clean myself up, then I'm going to put my t-shirt back on. I suggest that you at least put your pants on so that we don't really get caught like this. That might be hard to explain."

I hated to do it, but I reached down into the warm depths of the sleeping bag, again savoring the delightful odor of sex that lingered inside the bag, grabbed my cargo pants, and slid them back on. While I was at it, I also threw my t-shirt back on for good measure. Then, with most of the evidence of our new¬found sexual relationship neatly hidden, we cuddled back up together. Perhaps it was my imagination, but it actually seemed to be getting warmer outside of the sleeping bag after our lovemaking. Within minutes, I could no longer see my breath. I fell asleep to the gentle sound of Sarah's breathing.

I drifted off to sleep, sleeping more soundly than I had in months. There is something about the body's chemistry after sex that leads to peaceful sleep.

My only recollection from my dreams that night was of the purple-robed figure from my previous dream sitting comfortably in an elaborately carved wooden chair, snacking on grapes and sipping wine from an ornately-wrought goblet of burnished gold. "You have passed my test, as I knew you would, my friend. That wasn't so bad now, was it? Now sleep well. You will need all of your strength tomorrow." He smiled and winked at me. And, with that, my dreams blurred into blissfully restful darkness

I awoke the next morning with the dim light of sunrise just beginning to cast long shadows across the top of the tent. Sarah had fallen asleep with her head on my shoulder and a slender arm across my chest. She looked angelic and adorable sleeping there. The warmth and softness of my cousin's body against mine and the gentle sound of her breathing lulled me back into a state of half-sleep. I took a deep breath, savoring the subtle, comforting scent of the woman in my arms.

It felt good lying there with her, but it was much warmer this morning than it had been the previous night, and it was soon too hot for me to continue lying in the sleeping bag with her. Disturbing her as little as I could, I slipped out of the sleeping bag. Sarah stirred a little, and I couldn't resist giving her a light kiss on her lips. She smiled sweetly without opening her eyes. As I slipped my shoes on, I heard a van door and recognized the voices of my friends and family that had slept there.

As much frost as I was certain that I had seen inside the tent the night before, I expected that there would be a great deal of moisture inside of the tent that we would have to allow to dry out before we stored the tent for any length of time. Looking around, however, I didn't notice any dampness on the inside of the tent's walls. There might be dew on the outside of the tent, but the inside looked like it was ready to pack back into the plastic container we kept it in until the next time we needed it.

Someone was walking rapidly towards the tent. Looking towards the door that my sister had left partially open when she had vacated the tent last night, I saw

Diana's smiling face looking in at us. "Rise and shine!" Her cheerful voice filled the tent. "We've got coffee going on the campfire, and Erin and I are making bacon, eggs, and pancakes for everyone!"

Sarah yawned and stretched, and we both looked at Diana's intrusion with good-natured humor.

"We'll be out in a second," I said as my friend disappeared towards the campfire.

Sarah lay in the sleeping bag, not quite ready to get up just yet. I was fully dressed, and if my help wasn't needed with breakfast then there was no rush for me to leave the tent. I sat down beside my cousin. "So how did you sleep last night, Sarah? Are you still OK with what happened?" I asked her.

Sarah reached out and took my hand in hers. She spoke in a soft whisper that the other people outside of the tent wouldn't hear. "I slept great. And the next time that you and I are alone somewhere where we can have a reasonable degree of privacy again, I'll be happy to show you just exactly how OK I really am with everything that happened last night. So are you OK? No weird morning-after regrets about fucking your own cousin?"

"My only morning-after regret is that there's not enough time or privacy right now for an encore." I whispered back. Sarah smiled wickedly as she began unzipping her sleeping bag.

"Hey, John!" came Kim's voice from the direction of the van. "Give Sarah some privacy so that she can get dressed, or she'll be using you as an excuse to stay in that sleeping bag all day!"

Sarah chuckled and replied loud enough for everyone to hear her. "Yeah, John. Get out of the tent so that I can get dressed without you seeing me naked!"

I looked over at her. She wasn't wearing panties under her t-shirt, and she grinned wickedly as she flashed her pussy at me. I began to move towards her, but she quickly closed her legs. She cackled quietly as she gestured me away with a shooing motion. I began making my way over to the door of the tent as she dug through her suitcase choosing what to wear that day. I couldn't resist one last look back at the delicious curves of her bare backside as she bent over the suitcase, and I pondered my good fortune in having a cousin like Sarah.

Breakfast has always been my favorite meal while camping, and that morning was no exception. Diana is probably the best campfire cook that I have ever known, and breakfast was phenomenal. I sat beside Diana, and we discussed our plans for the night as she playfully rolled her bacon and eggs up in a pancake and ate her creation like a burrito.

We had about seven hours of driving ahead of us, so we could easily leave at 9:00 and be at Erin's parent's place at 4:30 at the latest. That would give us time to unpack, get settled in, and get briefed on the site. Assuming that we spent an hour at dinner, two hours on the walk¬through, and an hour setting up, we would be ready to start the investigation well before sunset at 8:00.

I tossed my paper plate and napkin onto the fire. Heather and Erin had already finished eating and started on the dishes, which consisted of our well-used cast-iron pans, our battered tin camping cups, and the silverware. I thanked Erin when she offered to take my dishes, then busied myself with helping to disassemble and stow the tent, folding up the camping chairs, and loading everything in the back of the van.

I had just finished using water from my canteen to brush my teeth when Heather approached me, looking nervous. "John, could you take a quick walk with me?"

The poor girl looked scared to death, and I wondered if she was backing out of the investigation. "Sure, Heather. I'll be right with you." I returned my canteen and toothbrush to my rucksack, then returned to Heather. "It's going to have to be a short walk. Everyone else looks like they're almost ready to leave. Now, before we go, you know that nobody's going to think any less of you if you want to back out of taking part in the investigation, right?"

"A short walk is fine," Heather said. Something was definitely unusual in the way she was acting. Her voice sounded out-of-breath, and her cheeks were flushed. "And I'm not backing out of the investigation. I just have something I need to talk to you about. Now, if you don't mind."

"Are you OK, Heather?" I asked in genuine concern. "Is this about the... "

"I promise, I really am fine. I just need to talk to you," Heather's voice was pleading. "Let's walk."

"Hey, Diane, Heather and I are going to be gone for a few minutes," I shouted at Diana even as Heather was leading me away. Diana responded with a wave in my direction. She was busy ensuring that the campfire was entirely out. I felt guilty about leaving when there was still work to be done getting ready to leave, but Heather clearly needed me.

Joining Heather, I let her lead me down the road. She was power-walking much more quickly than her usual unhurried pace, and I had to start out in a light jog for a few seconds in order to catch up with her as she headed down the reed-lined gravel road. After about a hundred meters, the road we were on met a larger paved road at a T-intersection. Heather still hadn't said anything, and I began worrying. I briefly remembered Sarah hearing someone outside of the tent the previous night, and my heart was pounding in my chest. Did Heather know what her sister and I had done together last night? How would she be likely to react if she did, and what would those actions mean for me and Sarah?

After we crossed the paved road, Heather surprised me by keeping on moving straight into the woods on the other side of the road. She isn't in the best of shape, and she was breathing heavily. I followed her into the woods, our feet making crunching, shuffling sounds in the fragrant brown leaves of the forest floor. She looked around. Seeing a large fallen log, she led me over to it. Taking a seat, she patted the log beside herself and gestured for me to join her.

"John," she asked, "When you saw your sister's tattoo last night, you looked like you might have already seen it. Had you seen her tattoo before then?" Heather was breathing hard, perhaps from exertion, perhaps from something else.

I felt a wave of relief wash over me. She wasn't talking about me and her sister. Still, it was an unusual question to lead someone into such a private area just to ask them, and the nervousness that showed in her voice as she asked it was even stranger. I thought briefly about how to answer her. Did my dream count? "Well, I suppose, sort of."

Heather nodded. My evasive reply appeared to satisfy her. "Yes, I suppose that I had sort of seen it before then, too." Her voice was hushed, pensive, and nervous. She reached out with a warm hand that was trembling slightly, and took my own hand into hers. Pulling my hand to herself, she held it gently in her lap. Nothing too bold. Nothing that either of us could say was outside of the boundaries of normal behavior between cousins and old, close friends. Still, it wasn't quite normal for us. "You know what's kind of funny, John? Both of us had seen that tattoo before somewhere. But when I asked Kim if she had shown it to anyone before last night, she said no. Not even you."

As we held hands, Heather turned her head and looked at me. Her piercing blue eyes met mine for a long moment. I could tell that she was thinking very carefully about how to word her next question. I met her gaze, and she looked away from me, unable to look me in the eyes. "John, did you and I... spend any special time together the night before last?"

The only time we had even seen each other at all the night before last would have been in our dream. Heather had to be referring to that, but the notion still seemed impossible. My breathing became heavier at the memory of our incestuous union as I nodded, but I worded my reply carefully. "Yes, we did. And as I promised you at the time, I will never forget it." Again, my words would only make sense if we had both somehow, impossibly, remembered sharing the same dream. My heart pounded in my chest as I remembered what her body had felt like during our forbidden lovemaking, and I could almost taste my cousin's kisses again as I remembered what it had been like to be inside of her. But still, the careful wording of my answer meant that, if necessary, I could still save myself from embarrassment by pretending that I was talking about something else entirely.

Immediately after I answered her, I knew that my fears that she and I were discussing two entirely different things were in vain. Her hand tightened around mine, and we looked at each other for a long moment. She was breathing so deeply that I was afraid that she would hyperventilate, her shoulders heaving with every breath and the perfect, pale skin of her cheeks flushed a deep mottled crimson. She looked me in the eyes, meeting and holding my gaze. She was smiling and laughing nervously, but a few tears rolled down her soft round cheeks. She was completely overcome with emotion.

"I'll never forget it, either." Heather's voice was quiet, choking on the power of the feelings that seemed to swell in her pounding heart. We stared at each other for a long minute, her hot hands clenching my own tight in her lap. "I'll never forget anything about it, and I'll never regret sharing that with you whether you're my own cousin or not." She chuckled nervously as she acknowledged the taboo nature of what we had done together.

"I love you, Heather." I whispered quietly. I had spoken those words to her a million times before, but this time they meant something entirely different. My heart was pounding in my chest as, for the first time in our waking lives, my cousin and and I moved to kiss each other in a manner that was more than an expression of innocent familial affection.

Our lips met for the first time in our waking life. Her sweet, round, familiar face was pressed hard against my own, our lips and mouths silently communicating a life's worth of pent-up love between us. We were blissfully drowning in an ocean that washed over us in sweet waves of tender passion. I tasted her sweet mint- flavored toothpaste as her tongue and mine hesitantly met. Both of us were nervous to be sharing the forbidden, incestuous kiss with our favorite cousin and childhood friend. Both of us knew that nothing would ever be the same between us again, and I doubted that either of us could believe that this was really happening. As we held each other close, our kisses soon gained in both confidence and passion. Soon, our lips sealed together in steamy bliss as we rejoiced in our shared love, kissing like a bride and her groom beneath a chapel of tall trees. Our breath soon had her glasses frosted with fog, and she giggled as she pulled them off and stuck them through the waistband of her pants as I leaned her back to rest on the log. My cousin and I held each other close, our tongues intertwining wetly, our arms stroking each others' backs, our lips moving sweetly together as we kissed one another as lovers. Golden sunlight shone down through the leaves, and somewhere nearby a songbird was cheerfully serenading the two new lovers. Moving my lips, I kissed her chin, her cheek, and moved my lips to her neck.

Moving my lips from her mouth, I kissed the side of her neck and she let out a sweet, quiet gasp. I continued planting light, fluttering kisses upon her neck as her body pressed against my own. She moved her legs to place one on each side of the tree trunk that we lay upon and pulled me on top of her between her now spread legs. I lay between her legs, supporting as much of my weight as I could on the log behind her and savoring the feeling of my favorite cousin's pelvis grinding against me as I continued kissing her neck. As our crotches pressed together, I could feel the line of her zipper rubbing against me through my pants, and the thought of what lay beneath her clothing had my penis as hard as forged steel. She inhaled audibly as she felt one of the hands that held her slide beneath her sweater and t-shirt to feel the soft, warm skin of her back beneath her clothing. The contact between my calloused hand and the soft skin of her back excited both of us even further, and our minds were clouded by a fog of passion as we continued rejoicing in our shared love beneath the leafy canopy of the beautiful old forest.

Her blue-jean covered pelvis ground hard against me as my beloved cousin's familiar voice poured out in a feverish whispered rush. "Sweetheart, tell me what we did together two nights ago! Please, tell me! I need to hear you say it!"

"We made love, Heather. And it was the sweeter than I ever thought that lovemaking could be." She uttered a high-pitched, inarticulate cry of joy at my words, pressing her mouth hard against mine in a sloppy, scalding-hot kiss that a week ago I never could have imagined we would have shared. "I have always loved you, Heather," I whispered after long minutes of delighting in the blissful kiss, "and that night, you showed me exactly how much you have always loved me." The erotic memories of making love to my sweet, innocent cousin had my cock straining at the crotch of my pants as though it might tear through them. I knew that even through our pants she could feel my hardness pressing against her sex as our bodies continued to grind together through our clothes. If only that clothing weren't there!

Heather's breathing came in ragged gasps. "Oh, my God. Oh, my God, Ohmygod!" she was whispering. My sweet, pretty cousin was so excited by our circumstances that I could sense that, even through our clothing, the contact between our genitals was about to bring her to orgasm. Her arms tightened around me with more strength than I thought that she possessed, and her pretty round face scrunched up as she let out an inarticulate gasp. Heather's hips thrust up at me and then froze, her body trembling. She pressed her mouth hard into the shoulder of my jacket to muffle her gasping scream of joy and pleasure as her arms clenched tightly around me.

For long minutes, Heather held me close in trembling arms as her deep, ragged breathing slowly began to return to something that sounded more normal. "Yes, Sweetheart, we made love to each other. Oh, God, you really were inside of me! I got to feel you leave part of yourself inside of me to combine with my essence and create something beautiful together. I got to feel what it was like to have you make me the mother of your child! I felt myself claim you as the father of my own child. I have never loved anyone more than you, cousin."

We kissed again. I wanted to add something to what she had just said and let her know just how special the experience had been to me, but I was too overcome with emotion to speak. For a long minute, we held each other in silence, savoring the feeling of each other's body against us. My hand was still against her bare back inside of her shirt and sweater, my hand near the clasp of her bra. I could almost feel her heart beat against my chest as our soft breaths washed over one another's face. Heather and I were each breathing in the comforting, familiar scent of our beloved cousin, and we were cherishing it even more than we ever had before.

Heather whispered to me, her words coming out in a rapid-fire torrent of speech as though she had either bottled them up inside of herself for far too long, or as though she was afraid that she would loose her nerve and never speak them at all if she didn't do it at this very moment. "Sarah was right. I have always been in love with you for as long as I can remember! Even when we were small children, I remember how sad I felt when Mom told me I couldn't ever marry you because we're related, and I have always believed that I could never have you. But two nights ago, I got to taste your kisses and hold your body against mine with nothing between us. I felt every detail of making love to you. I got to feel what it was like to share an orgasm with someone that I have always loved more than life itsself, and it was the most beautiful thing I've ever experienced! I woke up, and could almost still feel your body inside of me. Then, last night, I got up to go to the bathroom and I walked past the tent. I watched and listened as you had sex with Sarah, and I knew for certain that you have no qualms about real-life sex with a flesh and blood relative."

Heather pulled my face to hers, planting a wet, sultry kiss on my lips. "Even inside the sleeping bag, even in the darkness, I knew exactly what the two of you were doing.

I watched you give her what I have always wanted, and I'm not ashamed to tell you that I stood there and masturbated outside of the tent as I watched you. I knew that what you were doing with her was going to become a reality between us soon as well, cousin. Very soon. We would make love right now if they weren't waiting for us back at the van." Heather's hot lips brushed my own, teasingly. She kissed my neck, and I gasped. "If they weren't waiting for us, you could have me right here on this log. Maybe in the position we're in right now, or maybe I would be bent over the log with you taking me from behind. Maybe I would be straddling you as you lay in the leaves. Most likely, I think we would try a couple of positions until we found one that we decided was our favorite," my childhood friend whispered quietly in my ear, as though afraid that the magic of this moment was so delicate that even a loud word could shatter it. My head swam, and my mind was filled with remembered images of her sweet, nude body and my throbbing cock disappearing into the soft curls between her legs.

Heather's voice was a barely audible whisper, her breath hot against my ear. "I heard you tell Sarah last night that you didn't have a condom. Neither do I. And I'm not on the pill. As a matter of fact, I'm super-fertile right now. I felt myself ovulate last night. I'm pretty sure that even if the head of your penis so much as brushed against my vagina, if even a drop of your pre- cum got inside of me, I might get pregnant just from that. But if we had the time right now," Heather held me close, her voice quiet and strained with nervous emotion, "none of that would stop us! I felt you get me pregnant two nights ago, and it was the most amazing thing I've ever felt!

Cousin, I would make love to you until you came inside of me just like you did in the dream we had. We have always loved each other, cousin. We could always be together! We could live together like a husband and wife and raise our children together. But soon, no matter what else is going on, we're going to become more than the closest of friends and more than the most beloved of relatives." She kissed me again, her hot, sweet, breath washing my face with the scent of campfire smoke and minty toothpaste. "We've always been inseparably close, but we're going to add a completely new element to our love, and we will become even closer. We're going to feel what we shared together two nights ago again and again. And we are going to love each other for the rest of our lives."

We were both trembling. I couldn't believe that I had just heard those words come out of her mouth. Sweet, innocent, responsible Heather, who didn't like to go to parties and who had just gotten into graduate school with a 3.9 overall GPA, was willing risk everything for unprotected, forbidden, incestuous sex with her own cousin. She looked at me with wide, frightened, doe-like eyes, as though afraid of being rebuked or laughed at. Instead, I pulled her closer to me.

"I love you, Heather. And soon we will make love. I promise. But can we use some sort of protection? I'm not sure that our mothers will be as happy to have us make grandchildren for them right now as they seemed about the idea in our dream." I chuckled lightly.

She flashed her brilliant old familiar smile that I have seen a million times before and always loved. "Sure we can use protection. But you had best get some soon if you want us to use it. I've always been in love with you, but I thought that because I was your cousin you wouldn't have me. I've waited my whole life for this, and I don't want to wait another minute if I don't have to."

I could see in her eyes that she had told the truth. She would have let me make love to her then and there, without protection and while her body was at its most fertile. I knew that everyone else was waiting for us back at the van and would soon be wondering where we were, and I knew that if I made love to my sweet, beloved cousin there would almost certainly be serious, life-altering consequences for it. But I remembered what it had been like to make love to her two nights earlier. I remembered her beautiful, soft, chubby body as she gave herself to me, and I wanted nothing in the world more than to have sex with her then and there, to plant my seed deep inside of her and make her my own forever. I pulled her closer to me, savoring the feeling of the woman I loved in her arms. After a lifetime of seeing each other almost every day and sharing a million innocent and happy memories together, suddenly getting just a few more minutes alone with my cousin seemed like the promise of heaven. But I couldn't let myself get her pregnant. She would let me, but I couldn't do that to her. We had to go back to the van now, while we still had the willpower to stop this.

"I love you, Heather," I breathed quietly into her ear. I couldn't resist kissing her soft lips again. I doubt that I could ever get tired of kissing her lips. "But everyone else is waiting on us."

"OK," she whispered. But we still clung to each other, neither of us moving. Again, we moved to kiss one another on the lips. In soft, slow, sultry movements our moist lips moved together. My cock was straining hard against my pants as Heather's tongue and mine slowly caressed each other, and her hand reached down and gently stroked my hardness through my pants. I raised my hips to avoid crushing her hand between us as I gasped into her mouth, and she increased the pressure of her hand against my manhood. Then I felt her fingers on the zipper of my pants as we kissed even more passionately, our saliva being freely shared as our tongues writhed together. I heard and felt my zipper being slid open, the cool air greeting the hot flesh of my cock. Then, I felt my cousin's soft fingers gently reach inside my pants to caress the skin of my penis.

Our kisses became sloppy and animalistic as Heather freed my cock from my pants and ran her soft hand along its length. I didn't care if it was wrong. I didn't care if it was incest. I didn't care that people were probably waiting on us, and I didn't care that neither Heather nor I had any protection available to us and we weren't in a position to raise children together at this point in our lives. The thought of pulling out of her once we began to make love was unthinkable. All that mattered at that very moment was our all-consuming need to consummate our love, to feel myself bathed by the sexual fluids of my beautiful cousin as we expressed our desire and passion for one another in the most natural way we could.

As my beloved cousin stroked my naked cock in her warm, soft hand, I had two choices. I could end this now and protect both of our futures, or I could reach for the button of her pants. Once her pants were unfastened, I had no doubt what she and I would do together, and my heart leapt into my throat as I imagined what that would be. My hand seemed to move of its own volition towards her waist, and I felt the crotch of her jeans beneath my trembling fingers as she sighed sweetly into my mouth. Even through the thick denim, I could feel the heat and humidity rise from her excited sex as my fingers fumbled with the button at the top of her jeans. Those jeans were separating my cousin and I from what we wanted most in this world at that moment, and she raised her hips to give me easier access to the button and zipper that held them on her.

I had never wanted anything more in my entire life than to make passionate love to Heather then and there, consequences be damned. And if we had a child as a result, then we would love that baby and raise it as any couple would. But I couldn't stand the thought of her promising future going out the window. I loved her far too much.

After I broke our long kiss, I looked deep into her pleading, sparkling blue eyes. "We need to go back to the van, Heather," I said breathlessly.

"All right," she replied. Her voice was quiet as I sat up and tucked my manhood back into my pants As I looked into her sad eyes, I could almost see reflections of what we both wished could have happened between us there in that beautiful forest.

We held hands for a bit while walking back to the road.

"I'm glad that we did that, John. I've been wanting some time alone with you for the last two days, and I feel better now that you feel the same way towards me that I feel towards you. I was afraid that things between us were literally just a dream on my part."

"I'm glad, too, Heather." We smiled at each other, and squeezed each other's hand.

"You know that things are never going to be the same between us," Heather whispered. "But I hope that you know that, no matter what happens, I'll always love you more than anyone in the world."

"I'll always love you, too, cuz." I said with a grin.

Heather and I arrived back at the campsite just as everyone was finishing up a walk-through of the area to ensure that we hadn't left any belongings or garbage behind. Satisfied that we had left our campsite the way we had found it, we hit the road.

We still had several hours of driving ahead of us. I sat in the van in the back, between Diane and Heather. As the van made its way down the road, it gently rocked back and forth. Erin was driving, and from the front of the van some quiet Christian instrumental music was playing. We had scarcely driven for an hour when Heather lay her head on my shoulder and drifted into sleep. Her soft, warm body against mine and the soothing sound of her gentle breathing soon had me nodding gently in my seat. Diane glanced over at Heather and I with drowsy, heavy-lidded eyes. Without saying a word, she rested her head upon my other shoulder. Why were we so tired? Didn't we get enough sleep last night? And those were the last thoughts I had before I drifted into blissful unconsciousness.

I found myself with Diane and Heather in the familiar clearing, but now it was daytime outside. Brilliant yellow beams of sunlight filtered down through the green needles of the fragrant pine trees and danced upon the soft carpet of verdant grass. At the edge of the clearing, the massive trunks of pines the size of California redwoods towered up to the sky. Among the trees I saw tendrils of wild grape vines and ivy. The woods seemed full of a dense fog. Diane ventured towards the forest and stepped into the greenish-gray mist.

"Are we where I think we are?" Heather asked me with nervous excitement.

"I believe so!" I replied with a wicked grin.

Heather's soft blue eyes met mine as her mouth curled into a wicked smile. 'We're dreaming again, so you don't have to worry about getting me pregnant," she whispered quietly enough that Diana wouldn't hear her. "at least not in real life. Here, I'm probably already carrying your child!" She smiled giddily. "And, now, nobody is waiting for us." Looking around and seeing Diane's back disappear into the woods, Heather kissed me.

"Holy shit, this is the thickest fog I've ever seen!" Diane's voice came from the fog.

"I would not go much further, if I were you," came a deep baritone voice from nearby. "Diana, would you mind if I led you back to your friends?" I turned and saw the muscular, white-bearded form of Acratophorus gently leading Diana out of the woods by her hand. "In this world, you really can fall off of the edge of the planet into oblivion. Oh, don't look so alarmed. You're native to a different reality, and would simply awaken back in the van if that happened."

"Who are you, and where is this place?" Diana asked him.

"Forgive me," the god said with a dramatic bow to the ladies. "My name is Acratophorus, the Giver of Unmixed wine. You might have heard me referred to as Dionysus? Bacchus? Yes, I can see that you've heard those names before. Regardless of what you call me, I'm the god of wine and revelry. Never mind. I'm a god that hardly anyone worships anymore, despite the fact that your culture would be well-suited for it. There are mortal musicians that have been dead for several generations and still have more followers than I do, and there are far more people that have heard of the latest celebrity gossip in your world than have heard of me." He said the words with a merry twinkle in his eye and a good-natured chuckle at his own self¬deprecation. "It's nice to meet you, Heather. Anyone beloved of my friend John is dear to me as well. And it's a pleasure to meet John's other best friend as well, Diana. That's a lovely name, by the way. That's what the Romans called one of my half-sisters. She always preferred being called Artemis, but I think that Diana sounds much prettier."

"And this place? You should ask the local deity that I put in charge here what he wants to call it."

Acratophorus gestured towards me. "I made this little reality just for John, and here he has powers second only to mine, which effectively makes him the ruling god of this world since I have no intention of doing much with it. He can will things into and out of existence and do whatever he likes here, in exchange for a few tiny favors that I need him to do for me some time soon. This place is his, and the reason it's so small is because he hasn't yet had the opportunity to add on to it. As the god of this world, he can construct it in whatever manner pleases him. In just a moment, I'll leave you all alone to go explore... anything here that needs exploring, I suppose. But first, may I please talk to John in private for a moment? Here, John, follow me into the woods, but first I would like for you to think of a bench beside the ladies here. Any kind of bench. Get a picture in your mind of what you want. Yes, what you're visualizing will work wonderfully. Don't look so surprised that I can see what you're thinking, I'm a god! You know that. Now, just will the bench to exist."

Diana and Heather looked on in amazement as the silhouette of the bench that I had been visualizing appeared on the ground near them like shimmering, sparkling liquid gold. I gasped along with Diana and Heather as the ornately carved marble bench I had been visualizing appeared precisely where I had imagined it!

"Good, God, John! How the fuck did you do that?" Diana exclaimed gleefully.

I was just as surprised as the ladies and I looked behind myself and shrugged to my friend as Acratophorus took me by the elbow and led me off into the mist of the woods. We wandered through the ancient pine trees as the swirling gray-green mist closed thicker around us. Soon I could hardly see anything more than a foot away from myself.

"Yes, this should be far enough." Acratophorus stopped. Here, half-obscured by the mysterious fog, the ancient god regarded me gravely as he appeared to mysteriously float in nothingness. It reminded me of the primeval chaos of some ancient pagan creation story. "John, may I borrow your pocketknife for a moment?"

I gave him a questioning look, but seeing that no explanation appeared to be forthcoming I whipped out the large folding lock-blade that I had carried since I had been in the Army, and I flicked the long, meticulously-honed blade open as I handed it to him. He took it from me and held it in both hands for a long moment, looking intently at the blade and murmuring quietly in some strange foreign tongue. He most certainly wasn't speaking in English, and I doubted that he was even speaking in ancient Greek. For a moment the blade glowed a bright, yellowish white that seemed to radiate a rainbow-like aura through the mist around it like sunlight shining thorough a prism. As I watched in surprise and confusion, my knife gradually returned to its original appearance.

Acratophorus tested the edge with his thumb. "You certainly do like to keep a blade sharp. I haven't held a knife with an edge like this in quite some time." I smiled at the compliment. "Be careful with this thing," he admonished as he deftly flipped it into the air and caught it by the flat of the blade, handing it back to me. "Consider this the first of several treasures that I'll bless you with. Among other things, the blade can't break or get dull, here or anywhere else. You'll find that your knife now has other magical properties as well, but I'm afraid that I can't tell you about them at this point without the risk of causing both of us a great deal of trouble. I wish that I could tell you more, but I hope that you will come to understand everything soon. I can tell you to take good care of this knife and keep it close to you, because you're going to be doing a lot of good with it very soon. In particular, I can think of a few souls that have been suffering in darkness for a long time that are counting on you to help them, and your friends will need you as well."

The muscular old god looked at me grimly as he clapped me on the shoulder. His manner reminded me of some of my old Army buddies before dangerous missions. Some of them had clapped me on the shoulder just like the ancient god just did before we loaded into our vehicles and headed out. And some of those brave young men were now resting in military cemeteries. Taking me by the shoulder, Acratophorus led me back from the misty forest and into the sunlit clearing.

"I wish that I could stay and chat for a bit longer, because there's a lot that I do need to tell you and soon, but I am desperately needed elsewhere if my plans are to succeed. After centuries of boredom, I've suddenly found myself without a moment to spare. Well, I'll leave you, your friend, and your cousin in peace. Take all the time you want. Erin won't stop to refuel the van for another three hours, and the rest of your friends will be content to allow you and the ladies to sleep."

Diane and Heather both looked at Acratophorus as though they were about to ask him questions or say something when he began fading from sight. With a smile like the Cheshire Cat, Acratophorus disappeared into nothingness.

My friends looked at where the ancient god had stood and gaped at the empty space where he had stood only seconds before.

After a long moment of silence, Diane spoke rapidly to me in her excitement. "So, that guy is some ancient Greek god, and he gave you the powers of a god as well? What the fuck, buddy? You became a god in an alternate reality and didn't think that this was something that you should mention to your best friend? I shouldn't have to save up my beer money when you should be able to turn water into wine, right?" She chuckled gleefully. "So you just created this bench by willing it into existence, and that guy says that you can actually build an entire world just like that?"

"Well, Diane, how do you propose that I should have started a conversation with you on the whole 'I'm a god in another world but here it's all I can do to keep my car running' thing?"

Diane and Heather both laughed. "You know that I'm just messing with you, buddy!" Diane said.

"I suppose that I did make the bench there," I said thoughtfully, "but I've never willed a world into existence before. I would kind of like to put some thought into exactly what I would like to add on to this place before I do too much," I replied.

"As far a what to create, maybe a pretty little woodland stream with a cozy little cabin beside it?" Heather suggested. "Kind of like that painting that I've got hanging up in my room? Please? Think of it as a gift to me, and practice for whatever you feel like adding on later. And I wouldn't stress too much about the pressure of creating your own little world. I'm pretty sure we're all dreaming, which means that momentous decisions aren't something to worry much about. Plus, if you really are the ruling god of this place, then if you screw something up too badly I'm sure you'll be able to fix it, right?"

Diane chuckled. "While you're making the land, just remember to keep the volcanoes and earthquake- ridden fault zones to a minimum. When you're working on the flora and fauna, go light on things like mosquitoes and poison-ivy. And if things get too badly out of hand, remember that there isn't much that a nice cataclysmic flood can't fix. So, Heather, you really think we're all dreaming? I've never been in a dream that felt this real before! Everything around us looks, sounds, feels, and smells real to me, and we wouldn't really all be able to share a dream together, would we?" Diane walked over to Heather. "Can I pinch you?" she asked her playfully.

Heather never responded to the question, because we were interrupted by a brilliant flash of golden light that exploded from the woods. Old habits die hard, and both Diane and I dropped into low crouches at the sudden brightness. You can know on an intellectual level that you're in a safe pace, but it's hard for anyone that has been a veteran of close combat to ever truly feel safe again. Only Heather stood to feel the refreshing rush of warm air that flowed over us from the beautiful forest. There before us, we could see that the mist had receded from the woods. And, through the trees, just as I had envisioned it, was a merrily bubbling stream and a picturesque little stone cabin that was weathered and moss-covered as though it had been there for centuries. Diane and I followed Heather as she ran giddily towards the cabin. I couldn't help but watch her perfect butt bounce as she ran and remember our interactions from that morning.

Heather pulled the weathered oaken door open into a cozy single room with a large bed in one corner, not far from a large old-fashioned stone fireplace that had a crackling fire burning merrily in it. A small oil lamp flickered on the wooden table at the edge of the room.

Herbs were drying in bunches that hung down from nails in the rafters, lending a fragrant smell to the room. I walked into the cozy, dimly lit space.

"Well, welcome home, cousin!" I said with a smile, hoping to distract myself from my wicked thoughts. Here I was, with god-like powers and in the company of two beautiful women, both of whom I cared about deeply and both of whom cared deeply about me. I wouldn't use my powers to seduce them. But what if not using my powers to seduce them involved not visualizing what it would be like to make love to them or wishing for it? That would be easier said than done under any circumstances. And deliberate efforts to not think about seducing them had roughly the same effect as the old joke about "Try not to think about a pink elephant.".

"It's perfect!" Heather exclaimed gleefully as she admired the cabin. "Thanks, John!"

Diane gave Heather and I a funny look as Heather pulled me into a full kiss on the lips and I returned it, but my best friend was too polite to say anything.

"So," Diane began, "This really is a dream, right?"

"Well, kind of," I replied.

"And I'm dreaming it, right?" Diane said, staring at me.

"I suppose that all three of us are dreaming right now." I said.

"Sure," Diane said dismissively as she flopped back on the bed, her eyes squinted shut and her forehead knit as though she were trying to reason through a difficult problem in her head. "Well, I'm having the most realistic dream I've ever had before. I hope that neither of you mind if I'm going to try to change the content of the dream a bit."

Both Heather and I laughed at the intense concentration that was written on Diane's face. It was anyone's guess what she was trying to do, but nobody could fault her for lack of effort.

"Diane, I don't think that's going to work for you. Listen, buddy. I just made the cabin for Heather. Why don't you tell me what you want and I'll make it happen for you?" I offered.

"Fine," said Diana in a frustrated tone as she opened her eyes. "If this is going to be the most realistic dream I've ever had, then I would like for this to be a dream with some sex in it. I haven't gotten laid in ages, and ever since I made out with you last night I've been hornier than a dog in heat! If I can't fuck you in real life, then you had best fuck the living shit out of me here in this dream so that I can at least have something to think about the next chance I get to masturbate."

So much for not visualizing sex and wishing for it. But I took some relief from the fact that the ladies seemed interested in sex even outside of this reality, and Diana brought up the topic here.

"You know," Heather offered thoughtfully, "I've been thinking just about the same thing."

"But the only guy here is your cousin! Don't you think that you'll feel kind of weird when you wake up if you let yourself dream about sex with him? Run on and leave the two of us alone," Diana pleaded.

"I'm in love with him, and he feels the same way about me Doesn't it make sense? You know how much John and I have always meant to each other. And in regards to feeling weird after dreaming about sex with each other, John and I have had sex dreams before where we didn't just have sex, he actually got me pregnant, at least in this reality. And when we woke up, not only did we not feel weird about it, it actually led to John and I making out in real life this morning. And I just about got him to do it with me while we were awake."

Diana looked at us both with wide eyes. "Dude, you were making out with your own cousin?" she said in shock.

There was no sense in hiding what had happened from my best friend. And if Heather and I were in love, it was only a matter of time before we had to tell everyone.

"Yes, Diana. That's what our little walk was about. She's right. We were making out."

Diana grinned at us. "Now I know I'm dreaming." She squirmed on the bed as she contemplated the notion. "You know, that's actually kind of hot!" she said with a wicked, wide-eyed, excited smile.

"I'm in love with him, Diana," Heather repeated quietly. "Whether we're cousins or not, I'm in love with him."

Diane was silent for a long moment. "You know that I'm in love with him too, right?"

Heather didn't answer.

"Since this is all just a dream anyway, can we share him?" asked Diana pleadingly. The moment seemed filled with quiet tension.

"Ladies, don't I get a say in this?" I asked.

"NO!" they replied suddenly in laughing unison as they rolled over, pinning me to the bed from either side.

It was as though my question had magically dispelled the tension in the air.

"You and I are going to finish what we started last night!" Diana whispered hotly into my ear as she kissed the right side of my face and climbed on top of me, grinding the crotch of her blue jeans against my hard cock through my pants. "I'm on the pill, so there's nothing to worry about, and we've both waited way too long for this!"

I saw Heather stand up and fold her thick glasses, placing them on the rustic wooden table. I watched, mesmerized, as she pulled her pink sweater and white t-shirt over her head to reveal the soft flesh of her pale torso. She was beautiful in a rubensque, curvy manner that unmistakably marked her as a woman among women. She smirked at Diane with a cocky grin. "You're not going to finish what you started with him last night as long as you've got your pants on!" Heather said cheekily as she unzipped her blue jeans and slid them off of her smooth, shapely legs. Wearing only her socks, bra, and panties, she climbed back onto the bed and kissed me hotly, her sweet wet tongue in my mouth. This wasn't a mere kiss between cousins. This was a kiss between two people that had loved each other for a lifetime and were taking that pure, beautiful love that they already had to a sublime next level. "Besides, Diane, I've literally known him since we were babies together, and so I've waited a lot longer for this than you have. And I'm NOT on the pill, and I'm probably already pregnant with his child, at least in this little alternate reality we're in!"

I felt more than saw Diane stand up, and heard the sounds of clothing being shed. Then I felt my belt being unbuckled, and felt Diane pull my pants off. "Fine, Heather. You fuck him first. I'll watch him fuck his cousin before he fucks me. But after you're done with him, it's my turn."

Heather and I broke our kiss just long enough for me to shed my shirt. I was immediately aware of the warm softness of her feminine belly pressing against my abdomen, and the cool, smooth texture of her satin bra pressing against my chest. Reaching behind Heather, I

unfastened her bra with one hand. With the other, I reached down, feeling the supple curves of her ample buttocks through her soft cotton panties as she gasped into my mouth. I pulled her bra off, freeing her soft breasts. She sighed, a musical, high-pitched "Oh!" as I rolled her over and sucked one of her pink nipples into my mouth as my rock-hard cock ground against the crotch of her panties.

Heather rolled over, pulling me on top of her. Our mouths moved together, kissing with intense heat and passion, as my hand moved across the warm softness of her breasts, down the soft skin of her adorably chubby belly, down under the waist of her panties, and into the treasure that rested between her legs. She moaned into my mouth as I felt the moist lips of her vagina part to accept my touch to her most intimate region. Everything about my cousin's pussy was delicious heat, wetness, and sweetness. Everything about her body was delightful warmth and softness. Our mouths were moving intently together as she ground her slippery pussy against my hand.

Suddenly, Heather and I were startled to feel her panties jerked down her legs. "If you're going to finger your cousin in front of me, you should at least let me see it!" Diane whispered hotly as she pulled the soft cotton panties off of Heather, revealing the heart-shaped nest of curly dark-blonde hair that surrounded her genitals. "You know, I've always known that you and Heather were close, but somehow if you were fucking a cousin I would have expected it to be Sarah. Heather just seems too sweet and quiet to do something like that."

"I had sex with Sarah last night," I said with a grin in between kisses with Heather as my fingers moved inside of my cousin's slick pussy.

"So, John, how did your best friend end up being the only one around that wasn't getting some hard dick? Do you have any idea how horny I've been lately?" Diane asked with mock-annoyance.

I looked over at Diane. My beautiful best friend stood near the bed, completely nude. Her curvy, shapely body was a perfect combination of soft femininity and sturdy athleticism, and she was exquisitely beautiful. Her flawless white skin was delicately enhanced with beautiful, artistically executed tattoos that complemented her natural beauty. She smiled at me as she tossed Heather's panties into a corner. "Like what you see, John?" She said in a boldly husky voice. She ran her hand down to the dark, neatly trimmed pubic hair that framed the moist slit between her legs. "Good. Because our days of being just friends are over. Today, you're going to find out everything you've always wanted to know about your best friend's pussy. How does that make you feel?"

I couldn't answer, and I doubted that Diane really wanted or needed me to. The kisses between Heather and I were feverish, our hands frantically taking in every square inch of our lover's body. It took every bit of my self control not to remove the fingers that my sweet cousin had welcomed into her body, and replace them with my rock-hard cock. "Let me kiss you between your legs, Heather." I whispered breathlessly.

She nodded her assent, and soon I found myself between her wide feminine hips, my head between the supple flesh of her soft thighs as I eagerly lapped the honey from her moist slit. Her unruly pubic hair gently tickled my face, and I inhaled delightful lungfuls of Heather's sweet musk. Her scent intoxicated me with arousal as I buried my face in the wet deliciousness of her nether region. She had been so wet that her pubic hair had cool beads of moisture that I felt against my nose and lips as I licked and sucked at her heavenly pussy. I delighted in the delicate aroma of my own cousin's most intimate parts as I held her tender petals open, sometimes running my tongue up and down the insides of her moist pink slit, sometimes driving my tongue as deep as I could inside of her birth canal. Her sultry gasps and moans rewarded my efforts, urging me to please my oldest and dearest companion however I could. I carefully lubricated a finger with her sweet fluids, and reached inside of her, exulting in the feeling of the ridged texture of her inner body. I curled my finger upward inside of her, feeling a slightly rough patch of flesh on the top of her vaginal wall, and applied gently pressure downwards towards her pubic bone as I carefully licked and sucked at her vaginal opening and clitoris. Reaching around with my other hand, I gently traced a finger around the bottom of her clitoris, lightly massaging her perineum.

A thousand memories from the life that we had shared since birth flashed through my mind, reminding me of how much I had shared with Heather over the years and how much I loved her. My tongue traced delicate circles under the hood of her erect clitoris, lightly flicking her glistening pink nub while my fingers worked on her, inside and out. Her gasps were becoming increasingly frantic. "Oh my God!" she yelled as I went for broke and sucked her clitoris into my mouth, massaging it in a circular motion with the rough top of my tongue. "Ok!" She gasped as she came hard, her body wracked by convulsions and her hand tapping my shoulder as though she couldn't take any more.

There is something so beautiful that it's almost magical about the vaginal fluids of a fertile woman. Her natural nectar becomes thicker, richer. It is delightfully slick, like clear melted butter, but with the delicate muskiness of fine wine. It is rich with her natural pheromones, which can melt the hearts and resolve of even the strongest men. A scent that whispers of something safe, natural, nurturing, beautiful, and supremely desirable. As Heather's fluids bathed my tongue and her scent filled my lungs, I had never before felt such love and infatuation for any woman, or such need to claim her and be claimed by her.

As I gave my cousin's sensitive clit a break, I felt a hand wrap around my cock, and then I was shocked by a delicious, hot wetness that I felt engulf my manhood. Looking down, I saw that Diana was lying on her back with her head between my legs, sucking my hard cock deep into her throat. Her legs were spread and I could tell that her free hand was working frantically to please her sopping pussy. Diane's eyes were closed as her mouth moved over my rigid cock.

"Are you ready to go again?" I asked Heather as best as I could as Diane expertly sucked my engorged manhood. Heather nodded, and again I buried my face between her legs. I was sexually excited beyond what I had once believed was humanly possible, and based upon the amount of sweet nectar that greeted me between my cousin's legs I wasn't the only one that was experiencing unusual levels of arousal.

I ate her pussy like a man that had been dying of thirst drinking the clear, sweet water of a desert oasis, delicately tracing my tongue over and around the hood of her clitoris. I lapped and sucked between her legs, drinking her precious life-giving nectar, and delighting in the warm slickness of her sweet vagina, the tickle of her pubic hair against my face, and the texture of her swollen labia against my tongue. Her musk drove me mad with unspeakable desire. I needed to mate with this beautiful woman that I loved so much and that I had been blessed to have as a cousin. As these thoughts burned in my mind, I felt my best friend's mouth moving expertly along my manhood. My body was trembling, and I willed myself not to ejaculate deep into Diane's throat as as I licked my cousin's most intimate parts. I couldn't cum. Not yet.

Reaching beneath Heather, I felt the smooth pink skin between her pussy and the delicately puckered rosebud of her anus. I continued to eat her pussy as I gently traced a finger along the accessible portion of her butt crack, ever so gently running a finger around the outside of her forbidden hole as she thrust her pussy up at me. "Oh, my God! Oh, my God! Oh, cousin, I love you!" she shrieked. I felt her clenching my hand between the perfect softness of her glorious, milky- white butt-cheeks as she unleashed an unintelligible cry of ecstasy and came again in my mouth, blessing me with even more of her sweet fluid. I exulted in the taste of a woman that, if she was not already bearing my child in this world, would be doing so very soon.

I couldn't wait any longer to make love to my cousin. I hated to wipe the fluids from my mouth because they had come from Heather, but I knew that she would appreciate my kisses more if I did. I wiped my own mouth with a blanket, and then pulled my cock from Diane's mouth and positioned myself between Heather's legs. She nodded at me eagerly. My cock was soaked by Diane's saliva, and Heather was wetter than any woman I had ever seen before. With one gentle push, I was sheathed entirely in the slick, moist depths of her warm, tight, unprotected pussy. We both let out a gasp of relief as we received what our bodies so desperately craved.

"That's it, John!" Diana said with wild, excited eyes as she turned to watch Heather and I, my best friend's fingers working frantically between her legs. "Fuck your cousin! Fuck your own cousin without any protection and cum inside of her!"

The cabin was filled with the wet sounds of frantic copulation between my cousin and I. Heather and I mated, our mouths meeting together wetly in deep, passionate kisses, the soft plumpness of her ample belly making slapping sounds as my abdomen met it again and again. I felt the slick tightness of her vaginal walls clench possessively around my manhood even as I claimed her insides with deep thrusts. At that moment, Heather and I belonged to one another completely. "Oh, cousin!" Heather cried out. "Oh, cousin, I love you so much! Please, cum inside of me! I want you to make certain that I'm pregnant! Plant your love deep within me until my belly swells with our child! Oh, please, make me a mother! Oh, pleeeease... aaaaah!" She never finished the sentence. Her eyes rolled back into her head, and I felt the slick walls of her drenched birth canal clench hard around my cock.

Heather cried aloud as she experienced a mind-blowing orgasm. Her fingers tightened across my back and her soft legs clenched with all of her strength to pull me as deep into her trembling core as I could get. I could feel the tip of my hard penis pressed against her cervix, and knew that I was feeling her anatomical holy of holies, the most intimate part of her most intimate parts. Here was the entrance to her womb, the opening into the sacred chamber where the child that we would create together would grow. The slit at the head of my cock was sealed tightly against the natural portal that led from my cousin's vagina, through her cervix, and deep into her womb. If she wasn't already pregnant, just beyond that womb my sperm would find a ripe egg traveling down her fallopian tubes, and my cousin and I would be bonded together eternally as parents. As my beloved cousin's screams of inarticulate pleasure resounded within the cabin, I felt a hand lovingly and gently caress my testicles from behind.

"Cum inside of Heather, John. Make sure you've gotten your own cousin pregnant! God, I can't believe I get to watch this!" Diane whispered hotly as fingers that were slick with her own glistening moisture worked frantically between her shapely legs.

I felt like I was experiencing the creation of the universe. I felt my entire existence compressed into a singularity; all that existed was the act of fertilizing my beloved cousin's precious womb. And then that singularity exploded. "I love you, Heather! Yes, please let me be the father of your child! Please, cousin, have my baby!" I cried out as I felt the contractions begin within my own body, and I groaned with unspeakable pleasure as an ecstatic electricity filled my brain and washed over my entire body. Spurt after powerful liquid spurt erupted from my body deep into the fertile core of my cousin's drenched insides. I could almost feel her womb drinking my semen, sucking every drop that I could provide for the sacred purpose of creating life within her. Our orgasm seemed to last for ages, an all-consuming, mind-blowing experience that would be impossible to describe to anyone but the two of us who shared it.

Afterwords, I lay there, still sheathed deep inside of my cousin's hot, slick birth canal, and still rock-hard. My penis was still occasionally pulsing as my cousin and I continued to share our life-giving gifts with one another. "I love you, Heather," I whispered softly. Just a few weeks ago, I had known that Heather was the dearest human being in the world to me, but I had never taken even a moment to contemplate what it would be like to have her as a lover. Now that I knew what it was like to completely give my heart to someone that I trusted and loved completely, I couldn't imagine ever not having Heather as both my cousin and my lover. Perhaps even some day my wife and the mother of my children in the real world as well, no matter what anyone said about it.

"I love you, too." Heather whispered dreamily. She smiled beatifically as she lay beneath me, her pretty round face bathed in post-orgasmic bliss. "God, I feel so... I feel so complete! John, this is just so perfect!" she said as she kissed me. "But for now, you've got someone else waiting on you."

"You're sure you don't mind?" I asked Heather with some surprise. I didn't expect to have the energy to even move after an orgasm like that, but I recovered more quickly than I ever would have thought possible. I suppose that being a minor deity in an alternate reality has its perks.

"I don't mind!" Heather said. "She's your best friend, and a deal's a deal. I got to make love to you first, and now it's her turn."

I groaned painfully as I eased my sensitive cock from my cousin's slippery tunnel, and couldn't resist kissing Heather's soft lips again as I saw our mixed fluids trickling gently out of the sacred folds at the center of her vulva. I considered the implications of those warm, slippery fluids flowing together so freely. Our mixed fluids seemed to symbolize our merged hearts, and I felt hesitant to give myself to anyone but my cousin.

As I slowly moved away from my recently impregnated cousin, Diane grabbed me fiercely by the face and pulled me into a passionate kiss.

"She damned well had better not mind if we fuck, John! I've never been so horny before in my entire life! I can't believe how hot that was watching you knock up your own cousin, and I can't wait to have you fuck me senseless! No, stop right there, you had better not wipe your dick off! For one thing, that's an awesome antique quilt, not a rag from an auto-shop. But more importantly, I want to know what incest tastes like, and I want to know what the mixed juices of two cousins that have just made a baby together feel like inside of my cunt. God, I haven't had a decent fuck in ages. And now I'm going to get one from my best friend! What could make today any better?" Diane exclaimed as she pushed me back to rest my head between Heather's soft white thighs, the damp pubic hair of Heather's freshly- fucked pussy tickling my ear with moist tendrils. The comfortable scent of Heather's recently impregnated body filled my lungs.

Looking down, I saw Diane looking like a tattooed goddess as she bent over and ran her pink tongue over the tip of my cock. "Oh, my God. I love how you two taste!" Diane said as she licked her lips and smiled at me, but her soft hand continued to stroke my marble- hard penis. Then she bent over again, her dark hair brushing gently against my abdomen as she engulfed my cock, taking the entire length deep into her throat as she bobbed her head up and down. It felt amazing, but all too soon she stopped. "I thought that I would suck you off to get you hard again, but you're already more than there. I suppose that I just kept going because it was so awesome knowing what I was getting to taste. You and Heather are going to have to do this with me more often! So, what do you say, John? If you want to keep me in the friend-zone, you've got about two more seconds before I sit on that nice hard dick of yours and get the same treatment that you've been giving those pretty little cousins of yours!"

I struggled for something charming and witty to say, but was unable to speak a word before Diane had straddled my waist and positioned me at her opening. Leaning forward with her ample breasts pressing firmly against my chest, she kissed me deeply as her sweet pussy engulfed my member in steaming wetness. I had fantasized about this moment for years. I suppose that every guy that has a female best friend has thought more than once about what it would be like to know her sexually. Diane was giving me that precious gift, and it was more amazing than I had ever imagined. As our bodies undulated and writhed together I felt the hot, tight wetness of her underused opening sliding along the length of my manhood. Her lips caressed mine, our hands pulling each other's faces into a passionate kiss, our lips locking together as though made solely for that very act. Diana's pelvis and mine ground together, our pubic bones uniting firmly. I was suddenly aware that I felt my head rising and falling, and I realized that the motion wasn't from Diana. My head was resting in Heather's crotch, and she was now grinding her wet sex against Diane's hand, which in turn cradled my head. My cousin was using Diane's hand to masturbate, and I knew that if Heather came again after I had ejaculated inside of her, then her body would suck even more of my sperm into her fertile core. If possible, my rock- hard dick became even more firm inside of Diana.

Diane pulled her face away from mine and looked at me mischievously. "Wanna feel some reverse-cowgirl?" she asked.

"Sure!" I responded. As much as I hated to not be able to kiss her and appreciate my best friend's face and breasts, I looked forward to getting a better look at her shapely ass. Diana was a large-boned woman, but beautifully proportioned. I breathed in air that was thick with the delicate musk of lovemaking. It was the most beautiful scent I had ever known.

Diane climbed off of me and turned to give me a beautiful view of her gorgeous body from behind. I couldn't believe how perfect her butt was, and I admired the unmistakably feminine curves of her hips and waist. I had always known that Diane was a beautiful woman, and I will confess that I had tried to imagine her naked a thousand times over, but I was still amazed by how beautiful the actual sight of her nude body was. Positioning me at her opening, she slid down upon my shaft until the tip ground hard against her cervix. I couldn't believe how good she was at riding my cock; it was as though she knew me so well that she could anticipate precisely what I needed her to do to maximize my pleasure. I looked down as the soft, perfect globes of her ass undulated on my hips, her pussy massaging my cock to the brink of ecstasy. Up and down Diane's beautiful ass rose and fell, and I trembled with excitement as I watched time and time again as Diane's tight, wet pussy engulfed my member, only to slide back up leaving my cock glistening with her inner moisture. I knew that I couldn't hold off for long if she kept this up.

Diane cried out with a squeal of mock-alarm as I sat up and pushed her forward onto her hands and knees. Fucking her doggy-style would give me the control of the rhythm that I needed to hold off as long as I could. As I pounded hard into her soaked pussy, I reached around her and ran my hand over her sopping vulva. Moistening my fingers with her natural juices, I ran my warm, moist fingers around her sensitive clitoris, rubbing through the clitoral hod with controlled passion as I thrust my cock into her from behind with long, powerful strokes.

After several minutes of being stimulated inside and out, Diana grabbed the antique quilt and stuffed it into her own mouth as she let out a long, high-pitched shriek of sexual fulfillment. Her tight pussy spasmed and clenched around my manhood, and her body trembled in the throes of a massive orgasm. It was as though her strength was flowing out of her body as I pounded into her, and each thrust seemed to push her further into a position lying fully on her belly. Soon I was thrusting into her sweet pussy as she was lying face-down on the bed, feeling her delicious buttocks against my abs. And still she felt like she was cumming. I could no longer resist joining my beautiful best friend in orgasm, and so I let myself go. Waves of pleasure crashed over my overloaded senses as my rock-hard member ejaculated inside of her, unleashing a torrent of sperm deep within my best friend's body. Still she wiggled herself back at me, our bodies continuing to meet as her delicate pussy was milking my cock for every drop of cum that I could provide. Diana pressed back as hard as she could, grinding her ass rhythmically against me as I pushed forward, driving my spurting penis as deep into her as I could in this position.

I felt exhausted and light-headed, unable to move, and I collapsed on top of Diana's back, my cock still buried inside of her. I could still feel my penis occasionally pulse. I didn't know whether or not it was still spurting anything into her, but it still felt amazing just to remain encased inside of the moistness of her silken tunnel. Slowly, I grew soft inside of her, and I rolled off of her back and onto the bed. Soon I was joined by Heather and Diana on either side of me in a sweet post-orgasmic cuddle. Our bodies were as satisfied as they could get, and the beautiful naked women felt heavenly against me. I felt tired, and I briefly wondered what would happen if we fell asleep like that. After all, we were already asleep and dreaming.

I gradually eased into consciousness as the van was moving through Bennington, Vermont. Erin was still driving, and another CD of gospel music was playing softly. A few minutes later I felt Diane stir beside me. She smiled at me as she stretched and yawned.

"Have some sweet dreams?" I asked with a grin.

"Oh, you have no idea!" she said with a wicked smile before turning to look out the window. If she didn't think that I had any idea about her dreams, she clearly didn't understand what had just occurred. I looked down at the crotch of her blue jeans as surreptitiously as I could. She had more than soaked through the denim. Maybe I had just cum twice in an alternate reality, but here my cock leapt to full attention.

Heather awakened with a sweet moan beside me. I was probably the only one in the van that noticed the erotic undercurrents of that sound. I felt her almost imperceptibly move her lips as she tried to conceal the act of kissing my shoulder. "Thanks, John. That was amazing. But, like I told you this morning, we're going to have to do that in real life some time, and soon."

Diane heard Heather and gave her a shocked look, and Heather returned it knowingly. I smiled at Diane and nodded, as though confirming her unspoken query. Diane started to speak, but then thought better of it. Clearly flustered, she reached into her purse and pulled out a paperback and began reading it for a moment as though to distract herself and buy her some time to think, but she quickly realized that the romance novel was probably not going to help her to get herself under control. With shaking hands, she put the book back in her purse and watched as the pretty Vermont scenery filed past us. It took a lot to fluster Diana. I chuckled to myself as I turned to look out the window. Again, Diana started to move her mouth as if to ask Heather and I a question, but only gave voice to something that was less than a single syllable.

"Yes, what just happened was all real. Just in another reality." Heather spoke to her. "And John and I experienced it too."

Diane looked at her with her mouth agape and her pretty blue eyes as wide as saucers, but said nothing for a long time. "John, I... uh, Heather..." She clearly had no idea what to say to us. Finally she just whispered a quiet "Thank you both. That was incredible."

"What are you guys talking about?" Asked Kim from behind us.

"Nothing at all." Heather replied nonchalantly as she looked serenely out the window.

THE END.